Made possible

by a donation

from the

Thomas W. Kim Fund for Japanese

1998

RETOLD CLASSIC NOVELS

RETOLD CLASSIC: HUCKLEBERRY FINN

RETOLD CLASSIC: THE RED BADGE OF COURAGE

RETOLD CLASSIC: THE SCARLET LETTER

Perfection Learning, Logan, Iowa 51546

WRITER

Wim Coleman
M.A.T. English and Education
Educational Writer

CONSULTANTS

Rhonda Fey
Educational Consultant
Des Moines, Iowa

Gretchen Kauffman
Educational Consultant
Des Moines, Iowa

Dr. Jona Mann
Educational Consultant
Madrid, Iowa

Lois Markham
Educational Writer
Beverly, Massachusetts

REVIEWERS

Jim Fields
Tates Creek High School
Lexington, Kentucky

Pamela Friedman
Reading Consultant
Alameda, California

Ken Holmes
Lincoln High School
East St. Louis, Illinois

RETOLD CLASSIC NOVELS

RETOLD CLASSIC NOVEL
THE RED BADGE
OF COURAGE

by Stephen Crane

PERFECTION LEARNING

Editor-in-Chief:
Kathleen Myers

Managing Editor:
Beth Obermiller

Senior Editor:
Marsha James

Editors:
Randy Jedele
Christine LePorte

Cover Art: Douglas Knutson
Book Design: Dea Marks
Inside Illustration: Douglas Knutson

TABLE

OF CONTENTS

WELCOME TO THE RETOLD CLASSIC THE RED BADGE OF COURAGE

Henry Fleming's struggle to understand the meaning of courage has made Stephen Crane's *The Red Badge of Courage* an American classic.

We call something a classic when it is so meaningful that it is saved and passed down to new generations. Classics have been around for a long time, but they're not dusty or out-of-date. That's because they are brought back to life by each new person who reads them.

The Red Badge of Courage is a novel written years ago that continues to influence readers today. The story offers an exciting plot, important themes, fascinating characters, and powerful language. This is a timeless story about human emotions and experiences.

RETOLD UPDATE

This book is different from Crane's original story in two ways.

- Some chapters have been omitted. Brief summaries are provided for these parts so you can follow the complete story.

- The language has been updated. All the colorful and gripping details of the original story are here. But longer sentences and paragraphs have been split up. And some old words have been replaced with modern language.

In addition, a word list has been added at the beginning of each chapter. The list should make reading easier. Each word defined on the list is printed in dark type within the chapter. If you forget the meaning of a word while you're reading, just check the list to review the definition.

You'll also see footnotes at the bottom of some pages. These notes identify people or places. They also explain ideas or words that were common to Crane's time.

Also, at the beginning of the book, you'll find a little information about Stephen Crane. These revealing and interesting facts will give you insight into his life and work.

One last word. If you feel compelled to read the entire story, we encourage you to go to an original version to get more of Crane's rich imagery and interesting characterizations.

Now on to the novel. Remember, when you read this book, you bring the story back to life in today's world. We hope you'll discover why this novel has earned the right to be called an American classic.

Stephen Crane

INSIGHTS INTO STEPHEN CRANE

(1871-1900)

Crane was born in 1871 in Newark, New Jersey, the last of fourteen children.

Crane's father died when Stephen was just a child. Perhaps his early death explains why he didn't seem to have much influence on his son's outlook. Crane's father was a strict Methodist minister who frowned on many things. Crane, on the other hand, took up smoking, drinking, and swearing.

Reverend Crane even disapproved of reading novels. He would doubtless have been shocked to see his son become not just a reader but a writer of such books.

When Crane was a young man, his mother sensed that he was slipping away from religion. In desperation, she sent him to a religious training school founded by Crane's father.

But Crane disliked the school and ignored his studies. So his mother moved him to a school in Claverack, New York. There he "majored" in baseball, gambling, and swearing.

From Claverack, Crane went on to Lafayette College. But he flunked out after one semester.

At Syracuse University, Crane made one last try at completing a formal education. However, he spent more time playing baseball than going to classes. Not surprisingly, he dropped out after less than a year.

When Crane's attempts at formal schooling ended, his "real" education began. He got his start at a writing career by working as a cub (beginning) reporter for his brother's news service.

As a reporter, Crane's main job was gathering local gossip. This required that he closely examine the lives of common people.

continued

The habit of carefully observing people and their surroundings would stay with Crane throughout his life. So would his sympathies for the poor. When Crane later grew wealthy, he made a habit of offering a meal to any tramp who visited his house.

Crane learned even more about the struggle to survive when he moved to New York City. His experiences there among poor people moved him to pen his first novel, *Maggie: A Girl of the Streets.*

But Crane's brutal descriptions of poverty and violence proved too shocking for his time. No one wanted to publish the book.

Finally, Crane borrowed $700 from his brother and published the novel himself. But the book didn't sell well, leaving Crane discouraged.

The publication of *Maggie* did have some benefits. Two well-known writers of the time, Hamlin Garland and William Dean Howells, were impressed by Crane's style. They befriended the young author and continued to encourage him throughout his career.

Crane soon set to work on his second novel, this one about the Civil War. He completed the book in 1894 when he was 23.

Crane wrote this novel only to make money. Little did he know that the work, *The Red Badge of Courage,* would be judged his masterpiece.

Perhaps one of the most remarkable facts about *Red Badge* is that Crane wrote it without ever seeing combat. He based the book mainly on knowledge he gained from research. And he claimed that some of the book's most exciting battle scenes stemmed from his memories of playing football.

Crane also had trouble getting *Red Badge* published. At last, he found a newspaper willing to print it in serial form. Crane was so eager to see the book in print that he accepted the paper's low offer of ninety dollars.

A year later, in 1895, *Red Badge* was finally published

as an entire book. Critics loved the novel, and it became an immediate best-seller.

Crane was thrilled at his book's popularity. But he was a little uneasy about all the attention he received. He also felt that he could never top the success of *Red Badge*.

But this didn't keep Crane from writing. In the same year, he published a remarkable volume of poetry called *The Black Riders*. These verses proved Crane to be a talented poet as well as writer.

Though Crane is best known for his novels and short stories, he continued to write journalism pieces for most of his life. But even here, Crane felt that his talents went beyond just reporting the news. He liked to think that he captured emotions and feelings in his articles better than most journalists did.

In 1895, Crane accepted a job as a roving reporter in western America and Mexico. His lively articles about western life captured the public's attention.

While touring the West, Crane had some interesting adventures. Once he witnessed a bar fight between two men. Crane stepped in and tried to stop the fight.

Before he knew what was happening, a mob had dragged him before a judge, and Crane was charged with disturbing the peace! Since Crane was a stranger in the town, the charges were dropped. But the experience taught him something about life in the West.

Crane's western travels provided material for more than just newspaper articles. Several short stories—among them "The Bride Comes to Yellow Sky"—also sprang from his journeys.

When Crane returned to New York, he found himself caught up in a scandal. It began when he testified in court on behalf of a woman falsely accused of prostitution.

But in trying to help another person, Crane damaged his own name. Reporters already jealous of Crane's success seized the chance to spread gossip about him. They began falsely reporting that he used drugs and was involved in other

continued

immoral activities.

This negative publicity made it even harder for Crane to deal with his role as a famous writer.

An assignment to report on Cuba's war with Spain gave Crane some welcome relief. Eager to escape his troubles at home, Crane gladly took the job. He also wanted to see combat to determine if *Red Badge* was accurate.

However, Crane was not fated to get to Cuba on this trip. The ship he was on sank off the Florida coast. Crane spent thirty miserable hours in a lifeboat with several other people.

Though Crane survived, he never fully recovered physically. However, the experience did provide him with material for several works. Besides many newspaper accounts, his famous short story "The Open Boat" was inspired by the incident.

Crane finally received another chance to see combat. He and his lover, Cora Taylor, were sent to cover the war between Greece and Turkey.

Soon after he arrived on the scene, Crane became very ill. But with Taylor's help, he still managed to observe some battles. He was amazed at how accurately he had portrayed combat in *The Red Badge of Courage*.

After the war, Crane and Taylor moved to England. There they bought a huge house and lived in grand style. In fact, they spent more money than they could afford.

If Crane's lifestyle was richer in England, so was his circle of literary friends. He found his works were even more respected in England than in the U.S. Among the Britons who admired and befriended Crane were such famous authors as H. G. Wells, Henry James, and Joseph Conrad.

When war broke out between Cuba and the U.S., Crane at last got his chance to go to Cuba. In his role as a correspondent for a U.S. newspaper, Crane once again observed battle.

During this assignment, Crane sometimes acted recklessly.

Once he was with a group of men huddled in trenches. Suddenly, Crane stood up in full view of the enemy, who unleashed a round of bullets at him. Though no one was injured, Crane had put both himself and the men around him in extreme danger.

No one knows for sure why Crane took such a chance. It has been suggested that Crane knew he had tuberculosis—an often fatal disease at that time—and wished to end his life.

Later, Crane was sent to cover fighting in Puerto Rico. But the war was nearly over by then, and there wasn't much left to report.

Crane did have at least one strange adventure while in Puerto Rico. One morning he stole ahead of the American forces into the town of Juana Diaz.

When the townspeople saw Crane, they mistook him for a soldier. In minutes, all the troops in the village surrendered to Crane. Crane then proved what a generous "general" he was by leading the town in a celebration.

After his Puerto Rican assignment, it seems Crane decided not to return home. For a while, he disappeared in Cuba. Even Cora Taylor almost gave up trying to find him.

No one knows why Crane vanished. Some people believe that he knew he was dying and wanted to end his life alone.

Whatever the reason, Crane changed his mind when Taylor finally located him. The two returned to England.

Crane was constantly ill after his Cuban experience. But he continued to write, in part to pay off debts resulting from his free-spending lifestyle. However, neither critics nor the public responded warmly to these later works.

Finally, Cora Taylor placed the ailing Crane in a sanitarium (a hospital for long-term patients) in Germany. But he never regained his health, and he died at age 28.

Though Crane didn't even reach the age of 30, his writings had such impact that he is known as one of the world's classic authors.

continued

Other works by Crane
The Black Riders, poetry collection
"The Blue Hotel," short story
"The Bride Comes to Yellow Sky," short story
George's Mother, novel
Maggie: A Girl of the Streets, novel
"The Open Boat," short story

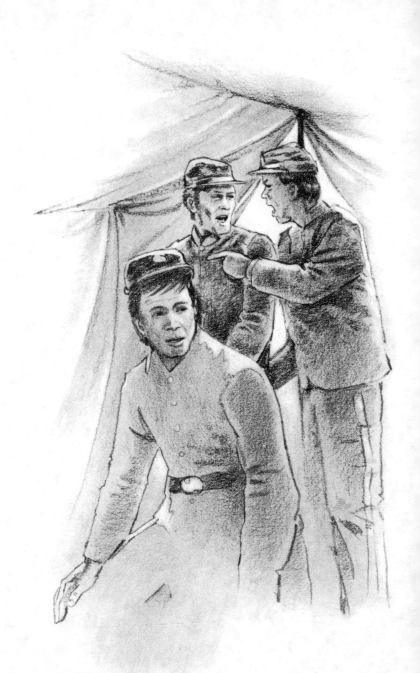

THE

RED BADGE
OF
COURAGE

STEPHEN CRANE

Chapter 1

The cold passed reluctantly from the earth. The fog lifted and revealed an army stretched out on the hills, resting. As the landscape changed from brown to green, the army awakened. It began to tremble with eagerness at the noise of rumors.

The army turned its eyes upon the roads. They were growing from long channels of liquid mud to proper roadways.

A river, brownish-yellow in the shadow of its banks, rippled at the army's feet. At night, the stream became a sorrowful blackness. Then one could see across it the red, eyelike gleam of enemy campfires set on the low brows of distant hills.

Once a certain tall soldier decided to do something worthwhile. He determinedly went to wash a shirt. Soon he came flying back from a brook, waving his shirt like a banner.

The soldier was full of a tale he had heard from a reliable

friend. The friend had heard it from a truthful cavalryman.[1] The cavalryman had heard it from his trustworthy brother, one of the orderlies at division[2] headquarters. The tall soldier put on the important manner of a messenger in red and gold.

"We're goin' to move tomorrow—sure," he said proudly to a group in the company street. "We're goin' away up the river. We'll cut across and come around in behind 'em."

For his interested audience, he described a loud and complicated plan of a very brilliant campaign.[3] When he finished, the blue-clothed men[4] scattered into small arguing groups between the rows of short brown huts.

A negro mule driver had been dancing upon a cracker box. But the forty soldiers who had laughingly cheered him on suddenly left him. He sat sadly down. Smoke drifted lazily from many quaint chimneys.

"It's a lie! That's all it is—a thunderin' lie!" said another private[5] loudly. His smooth face was flushed, and his hands were thrust angrily into his pants pockets. He took the matter as an insult to him.

"I don't believe the darned old army's ever going to move. We're set. I've got ready to move eight times in the last two weeks. But we ain't moved yet."

The tall soldier felt called upon to defend the truth of a rumor he himself had brought up. He and the loud one came near to fighting over it.

A corporal[6] began to swear before the crowd. He had just put a costly board floor in his house, he said. During the early spring, he had not added much to the comfort of his home. He had felt that the army might start on the march at any moment. Lately, however, he had started to believe that they would be camped forever.

Many of the men got caught up in a lively debate. One

---

[1]A cavalryman is a soldier who, at the time of this novel, was mounted on a horse.
[2]An orderly assists a higher-ranking military officer. For a definition of *division,* see the military chart on page 146.
[3]A campaign, in this case, is a series of planned military operations.
[4]The Union army of the North wore blue uniforms during the Civil War. The Confederate army of the South wore gray uniforms.
[5]See the military chart on page 147.
[6]See the military chart on page 147.

outlined, in an unusually clear manner, all the plans of the commanding general.

The general was opposed by other men. They claimed there were other plans of campaign. They shouted at each other. Many made useless attempts at getting the crowd's attention.

Meanwhile, the soldier who had fetched the rumor bustled about proudly. He was continually bombarded with questions.

"What's up, Jim?"

"The army's goin' to move."

"Ah, what you talkin' about? How you know it is?"

"Well, you can believe me or not, just as you like. I don't care a hang."

There was much food for thought in the way in which he replied. He came near to convincing them by refusing to prove what he said. They grew much excited over it.

There was a youthful private among them. He listened with eager ears to the words of the tall soldier and the many comments of his **comrades.**

After the youth had his fill of talk concerning marches and attacks, he went to his hut. He crawled through a complicated hole that served as a door. The youth wished to be alone with some new thoughts that had lately come to him.

He lay down on a wide bunk that stretched across the end of the room. In the other end, cracker boxes were made to serve as furniture. They were grouped around the fireplace. A picture from an illustrated weekly was upon the log walls, and three rifles hung parallel to each other on pegs.

Equipment hung in handy places. Some tin dishes lay upon a small pile of firewood. A folded tent was serving as a roof. The sunlight beat upon it from outside, making the roof glow a light yellow shade.

A small window shot a slanting square of whiter light upon the cluttered floor. The smoke from the fire at times missed the clay chimney and drifted into the room. This chimney, made from clay and sticks, was flimsy. It made endless threats to set the whole place on fire.

The youth was in a little **trance** of amazement. So they were at last going to fight. Tomorrow, perhaps, there would be a battle, and he would be in it. For a time he had to struggle to make himself believe it. He could not totally accept a sign that he was about to mingle in one of those great affairs of the earth.

He had, of course, dreamed of battles all his life. He had imagined unclear and bloody conflicts. They had thrilled him with their sweep and fire. In visions he had seen himself in many struggles. He had imagined others safe in the shadow of his eagle-eyed skill.

But awake, he had seen battles as red blotches on the pages of the past. He had thought of them as things of the bygone, like his thought-images of heavy crowns and high castles. There was a part of the world's history that he had thought of as the time of wars. But, he thought, this time had long gone over the horizon and had disappeared forever.

From his home, his youthful eyes had looked upon the war in his own country with distrust. It must be some sort of a game. For a long time, he had lost hope of witnessing a Greeklike struggle.[7] Such would be no more, he had said. Men were better—or more fearful. Worldly and religious education had put an end to the throat-grabbing **instinct.** Or else careful handling of money had held **passions** back.

He had burned several times to enlist. Tales of great movements shook the land. They might not be exactly Homeric, but there seemed to be much glory in them.

The youth had read of marches, sieges,[8] and conflicts. And he had longed to see it all. His busy mind had drawn for him large pictures. They were rich in color and glowing with breathless deeds.

But his mother had discouraged him. She had pretended to look with some disgust upon the quality of his love for war and patriotism. She would calmly seat herself. Then,

[7]*Greeklike struggle* refers to heroic battles in the *Iliad* and the *Odyssey,* both written by Homer. In these epic poems, war is a noble struggle between almost superhuman heroes. These heroes are constantly being helped by Greek gods.
[8]A siege is an army's attempt to take a specific target such as a city or a fort.

seemingly without difficulty, she told him why he was vastly more important on the farm than on the field of battle. She gave him many hundreds of reasons.

She had had certain ways of expression that told him that her statements came from deep beliefs. Moreover, on her side was his belief that her moral motive in the argument couldn't be argued against.

At last, however, he had firmly rebelled. He spoke out against this yellow light thrown upon the color of his ambitions. The newspapers, the village gossip, and his own dreams had aroused him to an uncontrollable point. The army was, in truth, fighting finely down there. Almost every day the newspapers printed accounts of a crushing victory.

One night he was lying in bed. The winds had carried to him the clanging of the church bell. Some excited person was jerking the rope wildly to tell the twisted news of a great battle.

This voice of the people rejoicing in the night had made him shiver in a long moment of excitement. Later, he had gone down to his mother's room and told her, "Ma, I'm going to enlist."

"Henry, don't you be a fool," his mother had replied. She had then covered her face with the quilt. There was an end to the matter for that night.

Nevertheless, the next morning he had gone to a town that was near his mother's farm. There he enlisted in a company that was forming. When he had returned home, his mother was milking the gray-streaked cow. Four others stood waiting.

"Ma, I've enlisted," he had said to her shyly. There was a short silence.

"The Lord's will be done, Henry," she had finally replied. Then she had continued to milk the gray-streaked cow.

Later he had stood in the doorway with his soldier's clothes on his back. There was a light of excitement and eagerness in his eyes that almost defeated the glow of regret for the home bonds. He had seen two tears leaving their trails on his mother's scarred cheeks.

Still, she had disappointed him. She had said nothing

whatever about returning with his shield or on it.[9] He had privately prepared himself for a beautiful scene. He had prepared certain sentences which he thought could be used with touching effect.

But her words destroyed his plans. She had stubbornly peeled potatoes and spoke to him as follows:

"You watch out, Henry. Take good care of yourself in this here fighting business. You watch out, and take good care of yourself.

"Don't go a-thinkin' you can lick the whole rebel army at the start, because you can't. You're just one little feller amongst a whole lot of others. You've got to keep quiet and do what they tell you. I know how you are, Henry.

"I've knit you eight pair of socks, Henry, and I've put in all your best shirts. I want my boy to be just as warm and comfortable as anybody in the army. Whenever they get holes in 'em, I want you to send 'em right-away back to me. Then I can darn 'em.

"And always be careful and choose your company. There's lots of bad men in the army, Henry. The army makes 'em wild. They like nothing better than the job of leading off a young feller like you. You ain't never been away from home much and you've always had a mother. But they'll be a-learnin' you to drink and swear.

"Keep clear of them folks, Henry. I don't want you to ever do anything, Henry, that you would be ashamed to let me know about. Just think as if I was a-watchin' you. Keep that in your mind always. Then I guess you'll come out about right.

"You must always remember your father, too, child. Remember he never drunk a drop of liquor in his life. And he seldom swore a cross word.

"I don't know what else to tell you, Henry. Excepting that you must never do no **shirking,** child, on my account. A time might come when you have to be killed or do a mean thing. And, Henry, don't think of anything except what's

---

[9]*Returning with [your] shield or on it* refers to a tradition of ancient Greece. Before battle, a mother would say this to her son. It meant he should return in victory or else die a hero, carried home upon his shield.

right. There's many a woman has to bear up against such things these times. The Lord'll take care of us all.

"Don't forget about the socks and the shirts, child. And I've put a cup of blackberry jam with your bundle. I know you like it above all things. Good-by, Henry. Watch out, and be a good boy."

He had, of course, been impatient while listening to this speech. It had not been quite what he expected, and he had listened to it with an air of irritation. He departed, feeling vague relief.

But then he had looked back from the gate. He had seen his mother kneeling among the potato peelings. Her brown face, upraised, was stained with tears. Her thin form was shaking.

He bowed his head and went on. Suddenly, he felt ashamed of his purposes.

From his home he had gone to his school to bid farewell to many schoolmates. They had crowded about him with wonder and admiration.

He had felt the difference now between them and had swelled with calm pride. He and some of his fellows who had on blue uniforms were quite overwhelmed with privileges for all of one afternoon. It had been a very delicious thing. They had strutted.

A certain light-haired girl had made lively fun at his military spirit. But there was another and darker girl whom he had gazed at steadily. He thought she grew bashful and sad at the sight of his blue and brass.

As he had walked down the path between the rows of oaks, he had turned his head. He spotted her at a window, watching his departure.

When he saw her, she had immediately begun to stare up through the high tree branches at the sky. He had seen a good deal of flurry and haste in her movement as she changed her position. He often thought of it.

On the way to Washington,[10] his spirit had soared. The

[10]During the Civil War, Northern troops went to Washington, D.C., before going south to fight.

regiment[11] was fed and well-treated at station after station. All of this had made the youth believe that he must be a hero. There was a rich spread of bread and cold meats, coffee, and pickles and cheese. He had warmed himself in the smiles of the girls and was patted and complimented by the old men. He had felt growing within him the strength to do mighty deeds of arms.

After complicated travels with many pauses, there had come months of boring life in a camp. He had had the belief that real war was a series of death struggles with a small time in between for sleep and meals. But since his regiment had come to the field, the army had done little. It simply sat still and tried to keep warm.

He was brought then slowly back to his old ideas. Greeklike struggles would be no more. Men were better— or more fearful. Worldly and religious education had put an end to the throat-grabbing instinct. Or else careful handling of money had held passions back.

He had grown to see himself merely as part of a vast blue demonstration. His concern was to look out, as far as he could, for his personal comfort. For fun he could twiddle his thumbs and guess at the thoughts which must trouble the minds of the generals. Also, he was drilled and drilled and reviewed, and drilled and drilled and reviewed.[12]

The only foes he had seen were some guards along the river bank. They were a suntanned, reflective lot who sometimes shot off-handedly at the blue guards.

When they were scolded for this afterward, they usually expressed sorrow. Then they swore by their gods that the guns had exploded without their permission.

The youth was on guard duty one night and talked across the stream with one of them. He was a slightly ragged man who spat skillfully between his shoes. He had a great amount of friendly and childish confidence. The youth liked him personally.

"Yank," the other had said to him, "you're a right damn

[11]See the military chart on page 146.
[12]*Reviewed* refers to the "formal inspection" of military troops. A review is usually done on a regular basis by officers of higher ranking than those being reviewed.

good feller.''

This thought floated to the youth on the still air. It had made him briefly regret war.

Various veterans had told him tales. Some talked of gray, bearded mobs who advanced with endless curses and chewed tobacco with unspeakable courage. These were great bodies of fierce soldiers who were sweeping along like the Huns.[13]

Others spoke of tattered and eternally hungry men who fired hopeless gunshots. ''They'll charge through hell's fire and brimstone[14] to get a hold of some food,'' he was told. ''And such stomachs ain't a-lastin' long.''

From the stories, the youth imagined red, live bones sticking out through slits in the faded uniforms.

Still, he could not completely believe in veterans' tales. Recruits were their victims. Veterans talked much of smoke, fire, and blood. But he could not tell how much might be lies. They always yelled ''Fresh fish!'' at him.[15] They were in no way to be trusted.

However, he understood now that it did not greatly matter what kind of soldiers he was going to fight. All that mattered was that they fought. No one argued against that fact.

There was a more serious problem. He lay in his bunk thinking upon it. He tried to mathematically prove to himself that he would not run from a battle.

Before, he had never felt required to wrestle too seriously with this question. In his life, he had taken certain things for granted. He had never challenged his belief in final success. And he bothered little about means and roads.

But here he was faced with a thing of concern. It had suddenly appeared to him that maybe in a battle he might run. As far as war was concerned, he knew nothing of himself. He was forced to admit this.

Some time before, he would have ignored the problem. He would have allowed it to kick its heels at the outer doors

---

[13]The Huns were fierce and warlike Asiatic people. They invaded Europe in the 4th and 5th century A.D.

[14]Brimstone is sulfur. Burning brimstone is traditionally connected with the fires of hell.

[15]*Fresh fish* means ''newcomer'' or ''beginner.'' It is like calling someone a ''greenhorn'' or a ''rookie.''

of his mind. But now he felt the need to give serious attention to it.

A little panic-fear grew in his mind. As his imagination went forward to a fight, he saw some ugly possibilities. He considered the creeping threats of the future. He failed in an effort to see himself standing bravely in the midst of them.

He recalled his visions of broken-bladed glory. But now as he stood in the shadow of the coming struggle, he guessed them to be impossible pictures.

He sprang from the bunk and began to pace nervously to and fro.

"Good Lord, what's the matter with me?" he said aloud.

He felt that in this crisis his laws of life were useless. Whatever he had learned about himself was here of no use. He was an unknown quantity.

He saw that he would again be forced to experiment, as he had done in early youth. He must gather information about himself. Meanwhile, he decided to remain close upon his guard. He must watch out for those qualities of which he knew nothing. He could not allow them to everlastingly disgrace him.

"Good Lord!" he repeated sadly.

After a time, the tall soldier slid easily through the hole. The loud private followed. They were arguing.

"That's all right," said the tall soldier as he entered. He waved his hand expressively. "You can believe me or not, just as you like. All you got to do is to sit down and wait as quiet as you can. Then pretty soon you'll find out I was right."

His comrade grunted stubbornly. For a moment, he seemed to be searching for a forceful reply.

Finally, he said, "Well, you don't know everything in the world, do you?"

"Didn't say I knew everything in the world," replied the other sharply. He began to pack various articles snugly into his knapsack.

The youth paused in his nervous walk. He looked down at the busy figure.

"Goin' to be a battle, sure, is there, Jim?" he asked.

"Of course there is," replied the tall soldier. "Of course there is. You just wait 'til tomorrow. You'll see one of the biggest battles ever was. You just wait."

"Thunder!" said the youth.

"Oh, you'll see fightin' this time, my boy. It'll be regular out-and-out fightin'," added the tall soldier. He had the air of a man who is about to hold a battle for the benefit of his friends.

"Huh!" said the loud one from a corner.

"Well," remarked the youth, "like as not, this story will turn out just like them others did."

"Not much it won't," replied the tall soldier, angered. "Not much it won't. Didn't the cavalry all start this morning?"

He glared about him. No one denied his statement. "The cavalry started this morning," he continued. "They say there ain't hardly any cavalry left in camp. They're goin' to Richmond, or some place, while we fight all the Johnnies.[16] It's some clever trick like that.

"The regiment's got orders, too. A feller seen 'em go to headquarters. He told me a little while ago. And they're raisin' blazes all over camp. Anybody can see that."

"Shucks!" said the loud one.

The youth remained silent for a time. At last he spoke to the tall soldier.

"Jim!"

"What?"

"How do you think the regiment will do?"

"Oh, they'll fight all right, I guess, after they once get into it," said the other with cold judgment. He made a fine use of the third person.[17] "There's been heaps of fun poked at 'em because they're new, of course, and all that. But they'll fight all right, I guess."

"Think any of the boys will run?" pressed the youth.

[16]Rebel soldiers were often called "Johnny" or "Johnny Reb." Union soldiers were nicknamed "Billy" or "Billy Yank."

[17]The tall soldier speaks in the third person when he uses "they" and "them" to refer to his own regiment. This is less personal than using "we" or "us" (first person).

"Oh, there may be a few of 'em run. There's them kind in every regiment, especially when they first goes under fire," said the other in an understanding way.

"Of course, it might happen that the whole kit-and-boodle might start and run. That is, if some big fightin' came first-off. Then again they might stay and fight like fun. But you can't bet on nothin'.

"Of course they ain't never been under fire yet," went on the tall soldier. "And it ain't likely they'll lick the whole rebel army all-to-once the first time. But I think they'll fight better than some, if worse than others.

"That's the way I figure. They call the regiment 'Fresh fish' and everything. But the boys come of good stock. Most of 'em will fight like sin after they once get shootin'," he added with a mighty stress on the last four words.

"Oh, you think you know—" began the loud soldier with **scorn.**

The other turned wildly upon him. They had an angry quarrel. They fastened upon each other many strange insults.

The youth at last interrupted them. "Did you ever think you might run yourself, Jim?" he asked. On ending the sentence, he laughed as if he had meant to aim a joke.

The loud soldier also giggled.

The tall private waved his hand. "Well," he said seriously, "I've thought it might get too hot for Jim Conklin in some of them battles. If a whole lot of boys started and run, why, I suppose I'd start and run.

"And if I once started to run, I'd run like the devil, and no mistake. But if everybody was a-standin' and a-fightin', why, I'd stand and fight. Be jiminey, I would. I'll bet on it."

"Huh!" said the loud one.

The youth of this tale felt thankful for these words of his comrade. He had feared that all of the untried men held a great and correct confidence. He was now somewhat reassured.

Chapter 2

Vocabulary Preview

Below is a list of words that appear in this chapter.
Review the list and get to know the words before
you read the chapter.

acute severe; strong
indignantly angrily
obscurity namelessness; unimportance
reproaches scoldings; criticisms
sarcasms taunts; mockeries
speculations guesses; thoughts or feelings

The next morning, the youth discovered the truth. His tall comrade had been the fast-flying messenger of a mistake.

Yesterday, some of the soldiers had firmly believed the tall soldier. But today, these same soldiers scoffed at him. There was even a little sneering by men who had never believed the rumor. The tall one fought with a man from Chatfield Corners[1] and beat him severely.

The youth felt, however, that his problem was in no way lifted from him. On the contrary, it was being drawn out unpleasantly. The tale had created in him a great concern for himself.

Now he had this newborn question in his mind. He was forced to sink back into his old place as part of a blue demonstration.

For days he made unending calculations. But they were all remarkably unsatisfactory. He found he could prove nothing.

[1]Chatfield Corners is in New York State. This regiment is from New York.

He finally concluded there was only one way to prove himself. That was to go into the blaze. Then he would watch his legs, so to speak, to discover their credits and faults.

He reluctantly admitted that he could not sit still with a mental slate and pencil. He would never come up with an answer that way. To gain it, he must have blaze, blood, and danger, even as a chemist requires this, that, and the other. So he worried for an opportunity.

Meanwhile, he continually tried to measure himself by his comrades. The tall soldier, for one, gave him some assurance. This man's quiet unconcern dealt the youth a measure of confidence. The youth had known him since childhood, and knew him very well. He did not see how the tall soldier could be capable of anything that was beyond him, the youth.

Still, he thought that his comrade might be mistaken about himself. Or, on the other hand, he might be a man doomed to peace and **obscurity** until now. But in reality, he may have been made to shine in war.

The youth would have liked to have discovered another who suspected himself. A sympathetic comparison of mental notes would have been a joy to him.

He occasionally tried to probe a comrade with tempting sentences. He looked about to find men in the proper mood.

All attempts failed. He could not bring forth any statement which looked in any way like what he wanted to hear. Nothing he heard sounded like a confession to those doubts which he privately admitted to himself.

He was afraid to speak openly of his concern. He dreaded to confide in someone dishonest who was upon the high plane of the unconfessed. From this elevation the youth could be criticized.

In regard to his companions, his mind wavered between two opinions. It depended on his mood. Sometimes he tended to believe them all heroes. In fact, he usually admitted in secret the superior development of the higher qualities in others.

He could imagine men going very quietly about the world, bearing a load of courage unseen. Although he had known many of his comrades through boyhood, he began to fear that his judgment of them had been blind.

Then, in other moments, he scoffed at these theories. He assured himself that his fellows were all privately wondering and shaking.

His emotions made him feel strange in the presence of men. They talked excitedly of a possible battle as of a drama they were about to witness. He could see nothing but eagerness and curiosity in their faces. It was often that he suspected them to be liars.

He did not pass such thoughts without thinking very badly of himself. He heaped **reproaches** on himself at times. He was convicted by himself of many shameful crimes against the gods of traditions.

In his great anxiety, his heart was continually protesting at what seemed to him the unbearable slowness of the generals. They seemed content to perch peacefully on the river bank. They left him bent down by the weight of a great problem.

He wanted it settled right away. He could not long bear such a load, he said. Sometimes his anger at the commanders reached an **acute** stage. He grumbled about the camp like a veteran.

One morning, however, he found himself in the ranks[2] of his prepared regiment. The men were whispering **speculations** and retelling the old rumors. In the gloom before the break of the day, their uniforms glowed a deep purple color.

From across the river, the red eyes were still peering. In the eastern sky there was a yellow patch like a rug laid for the feet of the coming sun. Against it, black and patternlike, loomed the gigantic figure of the colonel[3] on a gigantic horse.

From off in the darkness came the trampling of feet. The youth could occasionally see dark shadows that moved like monsters. The regiment stood at rest for what seemed a long time.

The youth grew impatient. It was unbearable, the way these affairs were managed. He wondered how long they

---

[2]A rank is a formation of soldiers marching side by side.
[3]See the military chart on page 147.

were to be kept waiting.

He looked all about him and thought about the mysterious gloom. He began to believe that, at any moment, the strange distance might be aflare. And the rolling crashes of battle might come to his ears.

Staring once at the red eyes across the river, he thought they were growing larger. They were like the eyes of a row of dragons advancing. He turned toward the colonel. He saw him lift his gigantic arm and calmly stroke his mustache.

At last, he heard a sound from along the road at the foot of the hill. It was the clatter of a horse's galloping hoofs. It must be the coming of orders.

He bent forward, scarcely breathing. The exciting clickety-click grew louder and louder. It seemed to be beating upon his soul. Soon a horseman with jangling equipment drew rein[4] before the colonel of the regiment. The two held a short, sharp-worded conversation. The men in the front ranks stretched their necks.

The horseman wheeled his animal and galloped away. He turned to shout over his shoulder, "Don't forget that box of cigars!" The colonel mumbled in reply. The youth wondered what a box of cigars had to do with war.

A moment later, the regiment went swinging off into the darkness. It was now like one of those moving monsters traveling with many feet. The air was heavy and cold with dew. A mass of wet grass, marched upon, rustled like silk.

There was an occasional flash and glimmer of steel from the backs of all these huge crawling reptiles. From the road came creakings and grumblings as some cranky guns were dragged away.

The men stumbled along, still muttering theories. There was a quiet debate. Once a man fell down. As he reached for his rifle, a comrade, unseeing, stepped upon his hand. He of the injured fingers swore bitterly and aloud. A low, giggling laugh went among his fellows.

Soon they passed into a roadway and marched forward with easy strides. A dark regiment moved before them. From

[4]*Draw rein* means "to stop a horse by pulling its reins."

behind also came the tinkle of equipments on the bodies of marching men.

The rushing yellow of the developing day went on behind their backs. The sunrays at last struck full and richly upon the earth. The youth saw that the landscape was streaked with two long, thin, black columns which disappeared on the brow of a hill in front. Rearward, the columns vanished in a wood. They were like two serpents crawling from the cavern of the night.

The river was not in view. The tall soldier burst into praises of what he thought to be his powers of insight.

Some of the tall one's companions cried out strongly. They said that they, too, had figured the same thing. They congratulated themselves upon it.

But there were others who said that the tall one's plan was not the true one at all. They stood firm in believing other theories. There was a heated discussion.

The youth took no part in them. As he walked along in the careless line, he was engaged in his own eternal debate. He could not stop himself from dwelling upon it. He was sad and disagreeable, and threw shifting glances about him. He looked ahead, often expecting to hear from the advance the rattle of firing.

But the long serpents crawled slowly from hill to hill without bluster of smoke. A grayish-brown cloud of dust floated away to the right. The sky overhead was of a fairy blue.

The youth studied the faces of his companions. He was ever on the watch to detect emotions like his. He suffered disappointment.

There was a kind of excitement in the air which was causing the veteran commands to move with glee—almost with song. It had infected the new regiment. The men began to speak of victory as a thing they knew.

Also, the tall soldier was proven right. They were certainly going to come around in behind the enemy. They expressed sympathy for that part of the army which had been left upon the river bank. They congratulated themselves upon being a part of the real war.

The youth considered himself as different from the others. He was saddened by the easy and merry speeches that went from rank to rank. The company fellows all made their best efforts. The regiment tramped to the tune of laughter.

The loud soldier let loose biting **sarcasms** aimed at the tall one. He often made whole files laugh without control.

And it was not long before all the men seemed to forget their mission. Whole brigades[5] grinned in unison, and regiments laughed.

A rather fat soldier attempted to steal a horse from a dooryard. He planned to load his knapsack upon it. He was escaping with his prize when a young girl rushed from the house. She grabbed the animal's mane. There followed an argument. The young girl, with pink cheeks and shining eyes, stood like a fearless statue.

The observant regiment stood at rest in the roadway. They whooped at once and entered whole-souled upon the side of the girl. The men became completely caught up in this affair. They entirely ceased to remember their own large war.

They jeered the piratelike private, and called attention to various faults in his personal appearance. They were wildly enthusiastic in support of the young girl.

To her, from some distance, came bold advice. "Hit him with a stick."

There were crows and catcalls showered upon him when he retreated without the horse. The regiment rejoiced at his downfall. Loud and noisy congratulations were showered upon the girl. She stood panting and regarding the troops with scorn.

At nightfall, the column broke into regimental pieces. These fragments went into the fields to camp. Tents sprang up like strange plants. Camp fires, like red, odd blossoms, dotted the night.

The youth kept from talking with his companions as much as circumstances would allow him. In the evening, he wandered a few paces into the gloom. From this little distance, he saw the many fires. The black forms of men passed to and fro before the red rays, making weird and devilish effects.

He lay down in the grass. The blades pressed tenderly against his cheek. The moon had been lighted and was hung in a treetop. The liquid stillness of the night surrounding him made him feel great pity for himself.

There was a pleasant touch in the soft winds. The whole mood of the darkness, he thought, was one of sympathy for himself in his distress.

He wished wholeheartedly that he was at home again. He wished he was making the endless rounds from the house to the barn, from the barn to the fields, from the fields to the barn, from the barn to the house.

He remembered he had often cursed the gray-streaked cow and her mates. And he had sometimes flung milking stools. But now he had a different point of view. He saw a halo of happiness about each of their heads. He would have sacrificed all the brass buttons on the continent to be able to return to the cows.

He told himself that he was not formed for a soldier. And he thought seriously upon the great differences between himself and the other men. They were dodging playfully around the fires.

As he thought, he heard the rustle of grass. He turned his head and discovered the loud soldier. He called out, "Oh, Wilson!"

Wilson approached and looked down. "Why, hello, Henry. Is it you? What you doing here?"

"Oh, thinkin'," said the youth.

The other sat down and carefully lighted his pipe. "You're gettin' blue, my boy. You're lookin' awfully pale. What the dickens is wrong with you?"

"Oh, nothin'," said the youth.

The loud soldier launched into the subject of the expected fight. "Oh, we've got 'em now!" he said.

As he spoke, his boyish face was surrounded in a gleeful smile. His voice had a joyful ring. "We've got 'em now. At last, by the eternal thunders, we'll lick 'em good!

"If the truth was known," he added, more soberly, "*they've* licked *us* about every clip up to now. But this time—this time—we'll lick 'em good!''

''I thought you was objectin' to this march a little while ago,'' said the youth coldly.

''Oh, it wasn't that,'' explained the other. ''I don't mind marching, if there's going to be fightin' at the end of it. What I hate is this gettin' moved here and moved there. No good comes of it, as far as I can see. We just get sore feet and damned short of rations.''[6]

''Well, Jim Conklin says we'll get plenty of fightin' this time.''

''He's right for once, I guess,'' said the loud soldier. ''But I can't see how it come. This time we're in for a big battle. We've got the best end of it, certain sure. Gee rod! How we will thump 'em!''

He arose and began to pace to and fro excitedly. The thrill of his enthusiasm made him walk with a spring in his step. He was spirited, vigorous, fiery in his belief in success. He looked into the future with clear, proud eyes. He swore with the air of an old soldier.

The youth watched him for a moment in silence. When he finally spoke, his voice was as bitter as dregs.[7]

''Oh, you're goin' to do great things, I suppose!''

The loud soldier blew a thoughtful cloud of smoke from his pipe.

''Oh, I don't know,'' he remarked with dignity. ''I don't know. I suppose I'll do as well as the rest. I'm goin' to try like thunder.'' He evidently complimented himself upon the modesty of this statement.

''How do you know you won't run when the time comes?'' asked the youth.

''Run?'' said the loud one. ''Run? Of course not!'' He laughed.

''Well,'' continued the youth, ''lots of good enough men have thought they was goin' to do great things before the fight. But when the time come, they skedaddled.''[8]

''Oh, that's all true, I suppose,'' replied the other. ''But

---

[6]Rations are the portions of food and water given to each soldier.
[7]Dregs are the particles and sediment that settle at the bottom of a liquid.
[8]*Skedaddle* means ''to run away.''

I'm not goin' to skedaddle. The man that bets on my run-nin' will lose his money, that's all." He nodded confidently.

"Oh, shucks!" said the youth. "You ain't the bravest man in the world, are you?"

"No, I ain't," exclaimed the loud soldier **indignantly.** "And I didn't say I was the bravest man in the world, neither. I said I was goin' to do my share of fighting. That's what I said.

"And I am, too," he went on. "Who are you, anyhow? You talk as if you thought you was Napoleon Bonaparte."[9] He glared at the youth for a moment. Then he strode away.

The youth called in a savage voice after his comrade. "Well, you needn't get mad about it!" But the other con-tinued on his way and made no reply.

The youth felt alone in space when his injured comrade had disappeared. He had failed to discover any likeness be-tween their viewpoints. This made him more miserable than before. No one seemed to be wrestling with such a terrific personal problem. He was a mental outcast.

He went slowly to his tent. He stretched himself on a blanket by the side of the snoring tall soldier. In the darkness, he saw visions of a thousand-tongued fear. It would babble at his back and cause him to flee. But others would go coolly about their country's business.

He admitted that he would not be able to cope with this monster. He felt that every nerve in his body would be an ear to hear the voices. The other men would remain deter-mined and deaf.

He sweated with the pain of these thoughts. He could hear low, quiet sentences. "I'll bid five." "Make it six." "Seven." "Seven goes."

He stared at the red, shivering reflection of a fire on the white wall of his tent. At last, exhausted and ill from the boredom of his suffering, he fell asleep.

[9]Napoleon Bonaparte (1769-1821) was born on the Mediterranean island of Cor-sica. He was a French general who eventually became Emperor of France.

Chapter 3

Vocabulary Preview

Below is a list of words that appear in this chapter.
Review the list and get to know the words before
you read the chapter.

Invulnerable safe; secure
ominous threatening; evil
perceived sensed; understood
solemnly grimly; gloomily
strenuously actively; intensely
trifle little; bit

Another night came. The columns, changed to purple
streaks, filed across two pontoon bridges.[1] A glaring fire
made the waters of the river look like wine. Its rays, shining upon the moving masses of troops, brought forth, here
and there, sudden gleams of silver or gold.

Upon the other shore, a dark and mysterious range of
hills was curved against the sky. The insect voices of the
night sang **solemnly.**

After this crossing, the youth assured himself that at any
moment they might be suddenly and fearfully attacked. Men
might come from the caves of the lowering woods. He kept
his eyes watchfully upon the darkness.

But his regiment went unthreatened to a camping place.
Its soldiers slept the brave sleep of wearied men. In the morning, they were awakened with early energy. They hustled

---

[1]Pontoon bridges are temporary floating structures used wherever a crossing is
necessary.

along a narrow road that led deep into the forest.

It was a rapid march. During it, the regiment lost many of the marks of a new command. The men had begun to count the miles upon their fingers, and they grew tired.

"Sore feet and damned short rations, that's all," said the loud soldier.

There were sweat and grumblings. After a time, they began to shed their knapsacks. Some tossed them down without concern. Others hid them carefully. They explained that they planned to return for them at some convenient time.

Men took off their thick shirts. Soon, few carried anything but their necessary clothing, blankets, food bags, canteens, and arms and ammunition.

"You can now eat and shoot," said the tall soldier to the youth. "That's all you want to do."

There was a sudden change from the heavy infantry of theory to the light and speedy infantry of practice. The regiment, relieved of a burden, moved faster now. But there was much loss of valuable knapsacks, and, on the whole, very good shirts.

But the regiment was not yet veteranlike in appearance. Veteran regiments in the army were likely to be very small groups of men.

Once, when the command had first come to the field, it met some marching veterans. These veterans noted the length of their column, and said to them, "Hey, fellers, what brigade is that?"

The men had replied that they formed a regiment and not a brigade. The older soldiers had laughed, and said, "O God!"

Also, their hats were too much alike. The hats of a regiment should properly represent the history of headgear for a period of years. And, moreover, the banners showed no letters of faded gold. They were new and beautiful. And the color bearer was in the habit of oiling the pole.

Soon, the army again sat down to think. The odor of the peaceful pines was in the men's nostrils. The sound of repeated axe blows rang through the forest. The insects, nodding upon their perches, sang like old women. The youth returned to his theory of a blue demonstration.

One gray dawn, however, he was kicked in the leg by the tall soldier. Then, before he was entirely awake, he found himself running down a wood road. He was in the midst of men who were panting from the effects of the speed.

His canteen banged rhythmically upon his thigh. His food bag bobbed softly. His musket[2] bounced a **trifle** from his shoulder at each stride. This movement made his cap feel uncertain on his head.

He could hear the men whisper jerky sentences:

"Say—what's all this—about?"

"What the thunder—we—skedaddlin' this way for?"

"Billie—keep off my feet. You run—like a cow."

And the loud soldier's shrill voice could be heard, "What the devil they in such a hurry for?"

The youth thought the damp fog of early morning moved from the rush of a great body of troops. From the distance came a sudden spatter of firing.

He was bewildered. As he ran with his comrades, he **strenuously** tried to think. But all he knew was that if he fell down, those coming behind would tread upon him. All his senses seemed to be needed to guide him over and past obstacles. He felt carried along by a mob.

The sun spread revealing rays. One by one, regiments burst into view like armed men just born of the earth.

The youth **perceived** that the time had come. He was about to be measured. For a moment, he felt like a babe in the face of his great trial. The flesh over his heart seemed very thin. He seized time to look about him carefully.

But he instantly saw that it would be impossible for him to escape from the regiment. It closed in on him. And there were iron laws of tradition and law on four sides. He was in a moving box.

As he perceived this fact, it occurred to him that he had never wished to come to the war. He had not enlisted of his free will. He had been dragged by the merciless govern-

[2]A musket is an old-style firearm.

ment. And now they were taking him out to be slaughtered.

The regiment slid down a bank and wallowed across a little stream. The mournful current moved slowly on. From the water, which was shaded black, some white bubble eyes looked at the men.

As they climbed the hill on the farther side, artillery[3] began to boom. Here the youth forgot many things as he felt a sudden burst of curiosity. He scrambled up the bank with a speed that a bloodthirsty man could not match.

He expected a battle scene.

There were some little fields surrounded and squeezed by a forest. Spread over the grass and in among the tree trunks, he could see knots and waving lines of skirmishers.[4] They were running hither and thither and firing at the landscape. A dark battle line lay upon a sunstruck clearing that gleamed orange color. A flag fluttered.

Other regiments struggled up the bank. The brigade was formed in line of battle. After a pause, it started slowly through the woods in the rear of the skirmishers, who were continually melting into the scene to appear again farther on. They were always busy as bees, deeply absorbed in their little combats.

The youth tried to observe everything. He did not use care to avoid trees and branches. His forgotten feet were constantly knocking against stones or getting entangled in briers.

He looked at these troops and their commotions. They were woven red and startling into the gentle fabric of softened greens and browns. It looked to be a wrong place for a battlefield.

The skirmishers in front fascinated him. They fired into thickets and at large and distant trees. They made him think of tragedies—hidden, mysterious, solemn.

Once the line came upon the body of a dead soldier. He lay upon his back, staring at the sky. He was dressed in an awkward suit of yellowish brown. The youth could see the soles of his shoes had been worn to the thinness of writing

---

[3] Artillery includes large, mounted guns such as cannons.
[4] A skirmish is a brief fight—too small to be a real battle. These skirmishers seem to be trying to kill stray enemy soldiers and snipers as the army marches forward.

paper. From a great tear in one, the dead foot poked out sadly.

It was as if fate had betrayed the soldier. In death, it exposed to his enemies his poverty. In life, he had perhaps hidden this poverty from his friends.

The ranks opened carefully to avoid the corpse. The **invulnerable** dead man forced a way for himself. The youth looked carefully at the pale face. The wind raised the brown beard. It moved as if a hand were stroking it.

The youth vaguely wanted to walk around and around the body and stare. The living sometimes try to read in dead eyes the answer to the Question.

The youth had been enthusiastic when out of the view of the field. But during the march, this feeling faded to nothing. His curiosity was quite easily satisfied. If an intense scene had caught him with its wild swing as he came to the top of the bank, he might have gone roaring on.

But this advance upon Nature was too calm. He had opportunity to reflect. He had time in which to wonder about himself and try to study his feelings.

Absurd ideas took hold upon him. He thought that he did not like the landscape. It threatened him. A coldness swept over his back. And it is true that his trousers felt to him that they were no fit for his legs at all.

A house stood peacefully in distant fields. To him, it had an **ominous** look. The shadows of the woods looked dangerous. He was certain that fierce-eyed enemies were hiding in this setting.

The swift thought came to him that the generals did not know what they were about. It was all a trap. Suddenly, those close forests would bristle with rifle barrels. Ironlike brigades would appear in the rear.

They were all going to be sacrificed. The generals were stupids. The enemy would soon swallow the whole command. He glared about him, expecting to see the sneaking approach of his death.

He thought that he must break from the ranks. He wanted to shout at his comrades. They must not all be killed like pigs. He was sure it would come to pass unless they were informed of these dangers.

The generals were idiots to send them marching into a regular pen. There was but one pair of eyes in the corps.[5] He would step forth and make a speech. Shrill and passionate words came to his lips.

The line was broken into moving fragments by the ground. It went calmly on through fields and woods. The youth looked at the men nearest him. He saw, for the most part, expressions of deep interest. It was as if they were studying something that had fascinated them.

One or two stepped with over-confident airs. It was as if they were already plunged into war. Others walked as upon thin ice. The greater part of the untested men appeared quiet and thoughtful. They were going to look at war, the red animal—war, the blood-swollen god. And they were deeply caught up in this march.

As he looked, the youth gripped his outcry at his throat. He saw that even if the men were shaking with fear, they would laugh at his warning. They would jeer at him. And if they could, they would throw objects at him. Admitting that he might be wrong, a noisy outcry of that kind would turn him into a worm.

He took on, then, the face of one who knows that he is doomed alone to unwritten responsibilities. He lagged behind, with tragic glances at the sky.

He was soon surprised by the young lieutenant[6] of his company, who began to heartily beat him with a sword. The lieutenant called out in a loud and unpleasant voice, "Come, young man, get up into ranks there. No creeping along will do here."

The youth stepped up his pace with suitable haste. And he hated the lieutenant, who had no appreciation of fine minds. The lieutenant was a mere brute.

After a time, the brigade was halted in the cathedral[7] light of the forest. The busy skirmishers were still popping. Through the paths of the wood could be seen the floating

[5]See the military chart on page 146.
[6]See the military chart on page 147.
[7]A cathedral is a large church.

smoke from their rifles. Sometimes it went up in little balls, white and compact.

During this halt, many men in the regiment began erecting tiny hills in front of them. They used stones, sticks, earth, and anything they thought might turn a bullet. Some built rather large ones. Others seemed content with little ones.

This activity caused a discussion among the men. Some wished to fight like duelists.[8] They believed it to be correct to stand straight. Then they could be, from their feet to their foreheads, a target. They said they scorned the ways of the cautious.

But the others scoffed in reply. They pointed to the veterans around them who were digging at the ground like terriers.

In a short time, there was quite a barricade along the regimental fronts. Directly, however, they were ordered to withdraw from that place.

This amazed the youth. He forgot his stewing over the advance movement. "Well, then, what did they march us out here for?" he demanded of the tall soldier.

His comrade with calm faith began a heavy explanation. He, too, had to leave his little protection of stones and dirt to which he had devoted much care and skill.

When the regiment was moved to another position, each man's thoughts for his safety caused another line of small barricades. They ate their noon meal behind a third one. They were moved from this one also. They were marched from place to place with seeming aimlessness.

The youth had been taught that a man became another thing in a battle. He saw his salvation in such a change. So this waiting was hard for him. He was in a fever of impatience. He thought there seemed to be a lack of purpose on the part of the generals. He began to complain to the tall soldier.

"I can't stand this much longer," he cried. "I don't see what good it does to make us wear out our legs for nothin'."

He wished to return to camp, knowing that this affair

---

[8] In a duel, two people stand face-to-face to fight one another to the death. Duels have been fought with swords and pistols, as well as other kinds of weapons.

was a blue demonstration. Or else he wanted to go into battle and discover that he had been a fool in his doubts. He wanted to learn that he was, in truth, a man of traditional courage. He felt the strain of the present circumstances to be unbearable.

The thoughtful tall soldier measured a sandwich of cracker and pork. He swallowed it in an offhand manner. "Oh, I suppose we must keep exploring the enemy country. We just got to keep 'em from getting too close, or to scout 'em, or something."

"Huh!" cried the loud soldier.

"Well," cried the youth, still fidgeting, "I'd rather do anything almost than go tramping around the country all day. We're doing no good to nobody and just tiring ourselves out."

"So would I," said the loud soldier. "It ain't right. I tell you if anybody with any sense was a-runnin' this army it—"

"Oh, shut up!" roared the tall private. "You little fool. You little damned cuss. You ain't had that there coat and them pants on for six months, and yet you talk as if—"

"Well, I want to do some fightin' anyway," interrupted the other. "I didn't come here to walk. I could have walked to home—around and around the barn, if I just wanted to walk."

The tall one, red-faced, swallowed another sandwich, as if taking poison in despair.

But gradually, as he chewed, his face became again quiet and contented. He could not rage in fierce argument in the presence of such sandwiches. During his meals, he always wore an air of happy enjoyment of the food he had swallowed. His spirit seemed then to join with the food itself.

The tall soldier accepted new environment and circumstances with great coolness. He ate from his food sack at every opportunity. On the march, he went along with the stride of a hunter. He objected neither to pace nor distance.

He had not raised his voice when he had been ordered away from three little protective piles of earth and stone. Each had been an engineering feat worthy of being made sacred to the name of his grandmother.

In the afternoon, the regiment went out over the same ground it had taken in the morning. The landscape then ceased to threaten the youth. He had been close to it and become familiar with it.

When, however, they began to pass into a new region, his old fears of stupidity and uselessness attacked him. But this time he doggedly let them babble. He was occupied with his problem. In his desperation, he concluded that the stupidity did not greatly matter.

Once he thought he had concluded that it would be better to get killed directly and end his troubles. He now looked at death out of the corner of his eye. He thought of it as nothing but rest. He was filled with a brief amazement that he should have made such a fuss over the simple matter of getting killed.

He would die. He would go to some place where he would be understood. It was useless to expect appreciation of his deep and fine senses from such men as the lieutenant. He must look to the grave for understanding.

The skirmish fire increased to a long clattering sound. With it was mingled far-away cheering. A battery[9] spoke.

Soon, the youth would see the skirmishers running. They were pursued by the sound of musketry fire. After a time, the hot, dangerous flashes of the rifles were visible.

Smoke clouds went slowly and boldly across the fields like watchful ghosts. The noise became louder, like the roar of an oncoming train.

A brigade ahead of them and on the right went into action with a terrible roar. It was as if it had exploded. After that, it lay stretched in the distance behind a long gray wall. One had to look twice to make sure that it was smoke.

The youth, forgetting his neat plan of getting killed, gazed spellbound. His eyes grew wide and busy with the action of the scene. His mouth was a little ways open.

Suddenly he felt a heavy and sad hand laid upon his

---

[9]A battery is an army unit equal in size to a company. (See the military chart on page 146.) A battery is equipped with the large guns and cannons used in battle.

shoulder. Awakening from his trance of observation, he turned and saw the loud soldier.

"It's my first and last battle, old boy," said the loud soldier, with terrible gloom. He was quite pale and his girlish lip was trembling.

"Eh?" murmured the youth in great amazement.

"It's my first and last battle, old boy," continued the loud soldier. "Something tells me—"

"What?"

"I'm a gone coon this first time and—and I w-want you to take these here things—to—my—folks." He ended in a trembling sob of pity for himself. He handed the youth a little packet done up in a yellow envelope.

"Why, what the devil—" began the youth again.

But the other gave him a glance as from the depths of a tomb. He raised his limp hand in a foretelling manner and turned away.

Chapter 4 (Summary)

The brigade stopped at the edge of a grove. The men crouched behind trees and pointed their guns at the fields.

Through the thick smoke they were able to spot men running. As they watched, they eagerly traded rumors with one another.

The noise in the fields swelled and became deafening. The youth and his companions watched in silence as a confused mass of men swarmed across the clearing. Bullets began to fly, and the group found themselves constantly ducking out of the way.

The youth's commanding lieutenant was shot in the hand. He swore so loudly that the men laughed nervously. The laughter relieved some of the men's tension.

More running men appeared out of the smoke. Soon it seemed that everyone was fleeing the battlefield. The flag fell as if giving up.

As the retreating men ran past the youth's regiment, veteran soldiers made fun of them. Their loud jeers were mixed with the whistling of bullets and shells.

The youth studied the frightened looks on the retreating soldiers' faces. The frantic men blindly struck anything within reach of their swords and fists. They seemed unconscious of the jokes of the veteran soldiers.

The youth felt overcome with fear. He knew that if he could only get himself to move, he would take off and run with the other men.

The youth realized he had not yet seen the made-up monster which had caused such terror among the retreating troops. But he felt he had to see it. Then he would probably outrun even the fastest men in his escape.

Chapter 5

There were moments of waiting. The youth thought of the village street at home before the arrival of the circus parade. It was a day in the spring.

He remembered how he had stood, a small, thrillful boy. He had been prepared to follow the dingy lady upon the white horse, or the band in its faded chariot. He saw the yellow road, the lines of waiting people, and the sober houses.

He particularly remembered one old fellow who used to sit upon a cracker box in front of the store. The old fellow would pretend to despise such displays. A thousand details of color and form came into the youth's mind. The old fellow upon the cracker box appeared more clearly than anything.

Someone cried, "Here they come!"

There was a rustling and muttering among the men. They displayed a **feverish** desire to have every possible cartridge ready to their hands. The boxes were pulled around into various positions and adjusted with great care. It was as if seven hundred new bonnets were being tried on.

The tall soldier, having prepared his rifle, produced a red handkerchief of some kind. He paid careful attention to its position as he knotted it about his throat. Then the cry was repeated up and down the line in a muffled roar of sound.

"Here they come! Here they come!" Gun locks clicked.

Across the smoke-filled fields came a brown swarm of running men who were giving shrill yells. They came on, stooping and swinging their rifles at all angles. A flag, tilted forward, sped near the front.

As he caught sight of them, the youth was briefly startled by a thought that perhaps his gun was not loaded. He stood trying to collect his weakening memory. He wanted to remember the moment when he had loaded, but he could not.

A hatless general pulled his dripping horse to a stand near the colonel of the 304th. He shook his fist in the other's face. "You've got to hold 'em back!" he shouted, savagely. "You've got to hold 'em back!"

In his **agitation,** the colonel began to stammer. "A-all r-right, General, all right, by God! We-we'll do our—we-we'll d-d-do—do our best, General."

The general made a passionate gesture and galloped away. The colonel, perhaps to relieve his feelings, began to scold like a wet parrot.

The youth turned swiftly. He wanted to make sure that the rear was not being attacked. He saw the commander regarding his men in a highly **resentful** manner. It was as if he regretted above everything his association with them.

The man at the youth's elbow was mumbling, as if to himself. "Oh, we're in for it now! Oh, we're in for it now!"

The captain of the company had been pacing excitedly to and fro in the rear. He coaxed in schoolmistress fashion, as if to a group of boys with primers.[1] He said the same things over and over again.

"Reserve your fire, boys—don't shoot till I tell you— save your fire—wait till they get close up—don't be damned fools—"

Sweat streamed down the youth's face, which was soiled like that of a weeping child. He frequently, with a nervous movement, wiped his eyes with his coat sleeve. His mouth

---

[1]Primers are small books used for teaching children to read.

was still a little ways open.

He got one glance at the foe-swarming field in front of him. He instantly ceased to debate the question of his gun being loaded. He wasn't ready to begin, and he hadn't announced to himself that he was about to fight. But he threw the obedient, well-balanced rifle into position anyway.

He fired a first wild shot. Immediately, he was working his weapon in an **automatic** way.

He suddenly lost concern for himself, and forgot to look at a threatening future. He became not a man but a member. He felt that the something of which he was a part—a regiment, an army, a cause, or a country—was in a crisis.

He was welded into a common personality, which was ruled by a single desire. For some moments he could not flee, no more than a little finger can run from a hand.

If he had thought the regiment was about to be destroyed, perhaps he could have amputated himself from it. But its noise gave him assurance.

The regiment was like a firework. Once lit, it would go higher and higher until its blazing life faded. It wheezed and banged with a mighty power. He pictured the ground before it as scattered with the wounded.

There was an awareness always of the presence of his comrades about him. He felt the **subtle** battle brotherhood. It was stronger even than the cause for which they were fighting. It was a mysterious kinship born of the smoke and danger of death.

He was at a task. He was like a carpenter who has made many boxes, making still another box. Only there was a furious haste in the youth's movements.

He, in his thought, was running off in other places. He was just like that same carpenter who, as he works, whistles and thinks of his friend or his enemy, his home or a saloon. And these jolted dreams were never perfect to him afterward. They remained a mass of blurred shapes.

Soon, he began to feel the effects of the war atmosphere. He came down with a blistering sweat. He had a sensation that his eyeballs were about to crack like hot stones. A burning roar filled his ears.

Following this came a red rage. He developed the sharp frustration of a pestered animal, a well-meaning cow worried by dogs. He had a mad feeling against his rifle, which could only be used against one life at a time.

He wished to rush forward and strangle with his fingers. He craved a power that would enable him to make a world-sweeping gesture and brush all back. His helplessness appeared to him and made his rage into that of a driven beast.

His anger was buried in the smoke of many rifles. It was not directed so much against the men who he knew were rushing toward him. Instead, his anger was directed against the swirling battle ghosts. They were choking him, stuffing their smoke robes down his parched throat.

He fought frantically for relief for his senses. He fought for air, as a babe being smothered attacks the deadly blankets.

There was a blare of heated rage mingled with a certain expression of watchfulness on all the faces. Many of the men were making low-toned noises with their mouths. These quiet cheers, snarls, curses, and prayers made a wild, savage song. It was an undercurrent of sound, strange and chantlike with the resounding chords of the war march.

The man at the youth's elbow was babbling. In it, there was something soft and tender, like a babe talking alone. The tall soldier was swearing in a loud voice. From his lips came a black stream of curious oaths.

All of a sudden, another broke out in a complaining way. He was like a man who has mislaid his hat. "Well, why don't they support us? Why don't they send support? Do they think—"

The youth in his battle sleep heard this as one who dozes hears.

There was a singular absence of heroic poses. The men, bending and surging in their haste and rage, were in every impossible position. The steel ramrods[2] clanked and clanged with endless noise as the men pounded them furiously into the hot rifle barrels.

[2]A ramrod is a long tool used to push ammunition down the barrel of a rifle.

The flaps of the cartridge boxes were all unfastened. They bobbed madly with each movement. The rifles, once loaded, were jerked to the shoulder and fired.

They fired without any real aim into the smoke or at one of the blurred and shifting forms. These forms had been growing larger and larger upon the field before the regiment. They were like puppets under a magician's hand.

The officers were spread out toward the rear. They forgot to stand in striking poses. They were bobbing to and fro, roaring directions and encouragements. The loudness of their howls was amazing. They used their lungs with mighty wills. They were anxious to observe the enemy on the other side of the tumbling smoke. Often they nearly stood upon their heads to do so.

The lieutenant of the youth's company had met with a fleeing soldier who was screaming at the first volley[3] of his comrades. Behind the lines these two were acting a little private scene.

The man was blubbering and staring with sheeplike eyes at the lieutenant, who had seized him by the collar and was beating him. The lieutenant drove the man back into the ranks with many blows. The soldier went mechanically, dully, with his animal-like eyes upon the officer.

Perhaps the soldier could hear a kind of godliness expressed in the voice of the lieutenant. The voice was stern, hard, with no trace of fear in it. He tried to reload his gun, but his shaking hands prevented. The lieutenant was obliged to assist him.

The men dropped here and there like bundles. The captain of the youth's company had been killed in an early part of the action. His body lay stretched out in the position of a tired man resting. But upon his face there was an astonished and sorrowful look. It was as if he thought some friend had done him an ill turn.

The babbling man was grazed by a shot that made the blood stream widely down his face. He clapped both hands to his head. "Oh!" he said, and ran.

[3]A volley is the firing of many weapons at the same time.

Another man grunted suddenly as if he had been struck y a club in the stomach. He sat down and gazed sorrowful-y. In his eyes, there was a silent, unspoken accusation.

Farther up the line, a man, standing behind a tree, had ιad his knee joint splintered by a ball. Immediately he had lropped his rifle and gripped the tree with both arms. And here he remained, clinging desperately and crying for help. Ηe wanted to withdraw his hold upon the tree.

At last a triumphant yell went along the quivering line. Γhe firing dwindled from an uproar to a last, cruel pop-ɔing. As the smoke slowly slipped away, the youth saw that the charge had been pushed back. The enemy was scattered into reluctant groups.

The youth saw a man climb to the top of the fence, strad-dle the rail, and fire a parting shot. The waves had departed. They left bits of dark rubbish upon the ground.

Some in the regiment began to whoop madly. Many were silent. Apparently they were trying to think about themselves.

After the fever left his veins, the youth thought that at last he was going to be smothered. He became aware of the foul atmosphere in which he had been struggling.

He was grimy and dripping, like a worker in a factory. He grasped his canteen and took a long swallow of the warmed water.

The same thing was being said up and down the line. ''Well, we've held 'em back. We've held 'em back, derned if we haven't.'' The men said it blissfully, looking at each other with dirty smiles.

The youth turned to look behind him and off to the right and to the left. He experienced the joy of a man who can finally relax enough to look about him.

Under foot there were a few **ghastly** forms that were mo-tionless. They lay twisted in fantastic shapes. Arms were bent and heads were turned in incredible ways. It seemed that the dead men must have fallen from some great height to get into such positions. They looked to be dumped out upon the ground from the sky.

From a position in the rear of the grove, a battery was

throwing shells over it. The flash of the guns startled the youth at first. He thought they were aimed directly at him.

Through the trees, he watched the black figures of the gunners as they worked swiftly and seriously. Their labor seemed a complicated thing. He wondered how they could remember how to do it in the midst of confusion.

The guns squatted in a row like savage chiefs. They argued with sudden violence. It was a grim pow-wow.[4] Their busy servants ran back and forth.

A small procession of wounded and depressed men went toward the rear. It was a flow of blood from the torn body of the brigade.

To the right and to the left were the dark lines of other troops. Far in front, he thought he could see lighter masses, sticking out in points from the forest. They hinted at unnumbered thousands.

Once he saw a tiny battery go dashing along the line of the horizon. The tiny riders were beating the tiny horses.

From a sloping hill came the sound of cheerings and clashes. Smoke swelled slowly through the leaves.

Batteries were speaking with thunderous, expressive effort. Here and there were flags, the red in the stripes standing out. They splashed bits of warm color upon the dark lines of troops. The youth felt the old thrill at the sight of the flags. They were like beautiful birds, strangely untouched in a storm.

He listened to the noise from the hillside. A deep, beating thunder came from afar to the left. Lesser noises came from many directions.

It occurred to him that they were fighting, too, over there, and over there, and over there. Before, he had supposed that all the battle was directly under his nose.

He gazed around him. The youth felt a flash of astonishment at the blue, pure sky and the sun gleaming on the trees and fields. It was surprising that Nature had gone peacefully on with her golden process in the midst of so much devilment.

[4]*Pow-wow* is taken from the Algonquian Indian word *pauwau,* meaning "medicine man." Here it is used to mean "conference" or "meeting."

Chapter 6 (Summary)

The youth woke up slowly and looked down at himself as if in a daze. It was almost like he had never really seen himself before.

It was over at last! The youth had passed his first trial of war.

Satisfaction flowed through his body. He recalled his efforts in the last battle scene and thought himself magnificent.

The youth felt a new closeness to his companions. He traded jokes and small talk with them.

Suddenly the peaceful atmosphere was broken by shouts of amazement: "Here they come again! Here they come again!"

The youth and his comrades groaned in disappointment. They looked up and beheld the enemy emerging from a far-off wood. The shells again began to whistle past.

The youth stared in disbelief. In his fatigue, he began to exaggerate the strength and skill of the enemy. He was astonished at their determination.

As the youth fired his musket, he became aware of a few men around him beginning to flee. With a yell of fright, the youth himself turned toward the rear and ran.

As he fled, he imagined he heard footsteps following close behind him. He thought the entire regiment must be fleeing.

The youth passed a brigade on its way to relieve the fighting troops. The fresh troops seemed unaware of the awful monster the youth was fleeing.

As the noise got farther away, the youth slowed. He came upon a general of a division on horseback.

The youth felt the general would call on him for information. But the general was unaware of the youth. The youth overheard him excitedly telling his staff that the men had held the enemy. He roared that the regiment would "whollop them" this time. The general's eyes shone with the desire to sing a hymn of victory.

Chapter 7

Vocabulary Preview

Below is a list of words that appear in this chapter. Review the list and get to know the words before you read the chapter.

brittle weak; breakable
conceived supposed; imagined
cringed winced; shrunk back
intricate twisted; tangled
melancholy sad; cheerless
strategy wise and careful planning

The youth **cringed** as if discovered in a crime. By heavens, they had won after all! The idiot line had remained and become victors. He could hear cheering.

He lifted himself upon his toes and looked in the direction of the fight. A yellow fog rolled about on the treetops. From beneath it came the clatter of musketry. Hoarse cries told of an advance.

He turned away amazed and angry. He felt that he had been wronged.

He had fled, he told himself, because destruction approached. He had done a good part in saving himself, who was a little piece of the army. He had considered the time, he said, to be one in which it was the duty of every little piece to rescue itself if possible.

Later the officers could fit the little pieces together again and make a battle front. If none of the little pieces were wise enough to save themselves from the flurry of death at such a time, why, then, where would be the army?

It was all plain that he had proceeded according to very correct and praiseworthy rules. His actions had been wise things. They had been full of **strategy**. They were the work of a master's legs.

Thoughts of his comrades came to him. The **brittle** blue line had withstood the blows and won. He grew bitter over it. It seemed the blind ignorance and stupidity of those little pieces had betrayed him. He had been overturned and crushed by their lack of sense in holding the position. Intelligent thought would have convinced them that it was impossible.

He, the wise man who looks afar into the dark, had fled because of his superior vision and knowledge. He felt a great anger against his comrades. He knew it could be proved that they had been fools.

He wondered what they would remark when later he appeared in camp. His mind heard howls of ridicule. Their fate would not allow them to understand his sharper point of view.

He began to pity himself severely. He was ill-used. He was trodden beneath the feet of an iron injustice. He had proceeded with wisdom and from the most righteous motives under heaven's blue. But he was only frustrated by hateful circumstances.

A dull, animal-like rebellion grew within him. It was against his fellows, war in general, and fate. He shambled along with bowed head, his brain in a confusion of pain and despair.

When he looked sadly up, quivering at each sound, his eyes had the expression of a criminal. His was the look of one who thinks his guilt and punishment great. And he knows that he can find no words.

He went from the fields into thick woods, as if determined to bury himself. He wished to get away from hearing the crackling shots, which were like voices to him.

The ground was cluttered with vines and bushes. The trees grew close and spread out like bouquets. He was obliged to force his way with much noise.

The creepers caught against his legs. They cried out harshly as their sprays were torn from the barks of trees. The swishing saplings tried to make known his presence to the world.

He could not make peace with the forest. As he made his way, it was always calling out complaints. When he separated embraces of trees and vines, the disturbed branches waved their arms and turned their face leaves toward him. He was afraid that these noisy motions and cries should bring men to look at him. So he went far, seeking dark and **intricate** places.

After a time the sound of musketry grew faint, and the cannon boomed in the distance. The sun, suddenly visible, blazed among the trees. The insects were making rhythmical noises. They seemed to be grinding their teeth in unison. A woodpecker stuck his bold head around the side of a tree. A bird flew on lighthearted wing.

Off was the rumble of death. It seemed now that Nature had no ears.

This landscape gave him assurance. A fair field holding life. It was the religion of peace. It would die if its timid eyes were compelled to see blood. He **conceived** Nature to be a woman with a deep hatred for tragedy.

He threw a pine cone at a cheerful squirrel, and he ran with chattering fear. High in a treetop he stopped. He poked his head cautiously from behind a branch and looked down with an air of alarm.

The youth felt triumphant at this display. There was the law, he said. Nature had given him a sign. The squirrel, immediately upon recognizing danger, had taken to his legs without a fuss. He did not stand bravely, baring his furry belly to the missile. He did not die with an upward glance at the sympathetic heavens.

On the contrary, he had fled as fast as his legs could carry him. And he was but an ordinary squirrel, too. Doubtless he was no philosopher of his race.

The youth wandered, feeling that Nature was of his mind. She backed up his arguments with proofs that lived where the sun shone.

Once he found himself almost into a swamp. He was obliged to walk upon bog tufts.[1] He had to watch his feet to keep from the oily mud.

He paused one time to look about him. He saw, out at some black water, a small animal pounce in and emerge directly with a gleaming fish.

The youth went again into the deep thickets. The brushed branches made a noise that drowned the sounds of cannon. He walked on, going from obscurity into promises of greater obscurity.

At length he reached a place where the high, arching boughs made a chapel. He softly pushed the green doors aside and entered. Pine needles were a gentle brown carpet. There was a religious half light.

Near the opening he stopped. He was horror-stricken at the sight of a thing.

He was being looked at by a dead man who was seated with his back against a columnlike tree. The corpse was dressed in a uniform that once had been blue. But now it was faded to a **melancholy** shade of green.

The eyes stared at the youth. They had changed to the dull color to be seen on the side of a dead fish. The mouth was open. Its red had changed to an awful yellow. Over the gray skin of the face ran little ants. One was lugging some sort of bundle along the upper lip.

The youth gave a shriek as he confronted the thing. He was for moments turned to stone before it. He remained staring into the liquid-looking eyes. The dead man and the living man exchanged a long look.

Then the youth cautiously put one hand behind him and brought it against a tree. Leaning upon this, he retreated, step by step. He kept his face toward the thing. He feared that if he turned his back, the body might spring up and sneakily pursue him.

The branches, pushing against him, threatened to throw him over upon it. His unguided feet were annoyingly caught

---

[1] A bog is wet, marshy ground. Here the youth is walking on small patches of grass to avoid the wet and muddy areas.

in brambles. With it all, he received a mysterious sugges-
tion to touch the corpse. As he thought of his hand upon
it, he shuddered terribly.

At last, he burst the bonds which had fastened him to
the spot and fled, paying no attention to the underbrush.
He was pursued by a sight of the black ants. He could see
them swarming greedily upon the gray face and approaching
horribly near to the eyes.

After a time he paused. Breathless and panting, he
listened. He imagined some strange voice would come from
the dead throat. He felt it would squawk after him in horrible
threats.

The trees about the door of the chapel moved like a
whisper in a soft wind. A sad silence was upon the little
guarding chamber.

Chapter 8

The trees began softly to sing a hymn of twilight. The sun sank until slanted bronze rays struck the forest. There was a lull in the noises of insects. It was as if they had bowed their beaks and were making a religious pause. There was silence, save for the chanted chorus of the trees.

Then, upon this stillness, there suddenly broke a tremendous **clangor** of sounds. A red roar came from the distance.

The youth stopped. He was held by this terrific joining of all noises. It was as if worlds were being torn. There was the ripping sound of musketry and the breaking crash of the artillery.

His mind flew in all directions. He imagined the two armies to be at each other panther fashion. He listened for a time. Then he began to run in the direction of the battle.

He had been at great pains to avoid the battle. And now he saw that it was an **ironical** thing for him to be running thus toward it. But he considered to himself what would happen if the earth and moon were about to clash. Many persons would doubtless plan to get upon the roofs to witness the collision.

As he ran, he became aware that the forest had stopped its music. It was as if it, at last, was becoming capable of hearing the foreign sounds. The trees hushed and stood motionless. Everything seemed to be listening to the crackle and clatter and ear-shaking thunder. The chorus rumbled over the still earth.

Something suddenly occurred to the youth. The fight in which he had been was, after all, but a half-hearted popping. In the hearing of this present noise, he was doubtful if he had seen real battle scenes. The uproar was like a battle of the stars. It was tumbling mobs a-struggle in the air.

He remembered a sort of humor in the point of view of himself and his fellows during the late encounter. They had taken themselves and the enemy very seriously. They had imagined they were deciding the war.

Individuals must have supposed they were cutting the letters of their names deep into everlasting tablets of brass. Or perhaps they thought they were placing their reputations forever in the hearts of their countrymen.

In fact, the affair would appear in printed reports under a meek and unimportant title. But he saw that it was good. Otherwise, he said, in battle every one would surely run, except those with lost hopes.

He went rapidly on. He wished to come to the edge of the forest so that he might peer out.

As he hurried, there passed through his mind pictures of tremendous conflicts. The thoughts he gathered together were used to form scenes. The noise was like the voice of an **eloquent** being, describing the scenes.

Sometimes the brambles formed chains and tried to hold him back. Trees met him, stretched out their arms, and forbade him to pass. The forest had been hostile before. Now this new opposition filled the youth with a fine bitterness. It seemed that Nature could not be quite ready to kill him.

But he stubbornly took roundabout ways. Soon, he was where he could see long gray walls of vapor. There lay battle lines.

The voices of cannons shook him. The musketry sounded in long, irregular surges. The sounds played havoc with his ears. He stood staring for a moment. His eyes had an awestruck expression. He gawked in the direction of the fight.

Soon, he started again on his forward way. The battle was like the grinding of an immense and terrible machine to him. Its puzzles and powers, its grim processes, fascinated him. He must go close and see it produce corpses.

He came to a fence and climbed over it. On the far side, the ground was littered with clothes and guns. A newspaper, folded up, lay in the dirt. A dead soldier was stretched with his face hidden in his arm. Farther off, there was a group of four or five corpses keeping mournful company. A hot sun had blazed upon the spot.

In this place, the youth felt he was an invader. This forgotten part of the battle ground was owned by the dead men. He hurried, with a kind of uneasiness. Perhaps one of the swollen forms would rise and tell him to begone.

He came finally to a road. He could see in the distance dark and agitated bodies of troops, smoke-fringed. In the lane was a blood-stained crowd streaming to the rear. The wounded men were cursing, groaning, and wailing. In the air, always, was a mighty swell of sound. It seemed to sway the earth.

There were brave words of the artillery and the spiteful sentences of the musketry. They mingled with red cheers. And from this region of noises came the steady current of the injured.

One of the wounded men had a shoeful of blood. He hopped like a schoolboy in a game. He was laughing hysterically.

One had been shot in the arm. He was swearing that it was because the commanding general had poorly managed the army.

One was marching with an air like that of some **sublime** drum major. Upon his face was an unholy mixture of happiness and pain. As he marched, he sang a bit of a tune in a high and quavering voice:

"Sing a song of victory,
    A pocketful of bullets,
Five and twenty dead men
    Baked in a—pie."

Parts of the procession limped and staggered to this tune.

Another man had the gray seal of death already upon his face. His lips were curled in hard lines and his teeth were clinched. His hands were bloody from where he had pressed them upon his wound. He seemed to be awaiting the moment when he should pitch headlong. He stalked like the ghost of a soldier. His eyes were burning with the power of a stare into the unknown.

There were some who proceeded **sullenly**. They were full of anger at their wounds, and ready to turn upon anything as a vague cause.

An officer was carried along by two privates. He was cross. "Don't joggle so, Johnson, you fool," he cried. "Think my leg is made of iron? If you can't carry me decent, put me down and let some one else do it."

He bellowed at the tottering crowd who blocked the quick march of his bearers. "Say, make way there, can't you? Make way, dickens take it all."

The crowd angrily parted and went to the roadsides. As he was carried past, they made smart remarks to him. He raged in reply and threatened them. They told him to be damned.

The shoulder of one of the tramping bearers knocked heavily against the ghostly soldier. He was the one who was staring into the unknown.

The youth joined this crowd and marched along with it. The torn bodies expressed the awful machinery that had entangled the men.

Orderlies and couriers[1] occasionally broke through the crowd in the roadway. They scattered wounded men right

[1]Couriers are messengers.

and left, galloping on and followed by howls.

The melancholy march was continually disturbed by the messengers. Sometimes it was disturbed by bustling batteries that came swinging and thumping down upon them. The officers shouted orders to clear the way.

There was a tattered man, fouled with dust, blood, and powder stain from hair to shoes. He trudged quietly at the youth's side. He was listening with eagerness and much **humility** to the shocking descriptions of a bearded sergeant.[2]

The tattered man's lean features wore an expression of awe and admiration. He was like a listener in a country store to wondrous tales told among the sugar barrels. He eyed the storyteller with unspeakable wonder. His mouth was hanging open in yokel fashion.[3]

The sergeant took note of this. He gave pause to his detailed history while he made a sarcastic comment. "Be careful, honey, you'll be a-catchin' flies," he said.

The tattered man shrank back, ashamed.

After a time he began to move sideways towards the youth. In a shy way, the tattered man tried to make him a friend. His voice was gentle as a girl's voice, and his eyes were pleading.

The youth saw with surprise that the soldier had two wounds. He had one in the head, bound with a blood-soaked rag. The other was in the arm, making that limb dangle like a broken branch.

They walked together for some time. Then the tattered man mustered enough courage to speak. "Was pretty good fight, wasn't it?" he timidly said.

The youth was deep in thought. He glanced up at the bloody and grim figure with its lamblike eyes. "What?" he said.

"Was pretty good fight, wasn't it?"

"Yes," said the youth shortly. He quickened his pace.

But the other hobbled quickly after him. There was an air of apology in his manner. But he seemed to think that he needed only to talk for a time. Then the youth would

[2]See the military chart on page 147.
[3]A yokel is a negative term for an ignorant country person.

see that he was a good fellow.

"Was pretty good fight, wasn't it?" he began in a small voice. Then he gained the courage to continue. "Dern me if I ever see fellers fight so. Lord, how they did fight! I knowed the boys'd like it when they once got square at it.

"The boys ain't had no fair chance up to now. But this time they showed what they was. I knowed it'd turn out this way. You can't lick them boys. No, sir! They're fighters, they be."

The tattered man breathed a deep breath of humble admiration. He had looked at the youth for encouragement several times. He received none, but gradually he seemed to get caught up in his subject.

"I was talkin' across pickets with a boy from Georgia, once. That boy, he says, 'Your fellers will run like hell when they once hear a gun,' he says.

" 'Maybe they will,' I says, 'but I don't believe none of it,' I says. 'And by jiminey,' I says back to him, 'maybe your fellers will run like hell when they once hear a gun,' I says. He laughed. Well, they didn't run today, did they, hey? No, sir! They fought, and fought, and fought."

His homely face was surrounded with a light of love. The army was to him all things beautiful and powerful.

After a time he turned to the youth. "Where you hit, ol' boy?" he asked in a brotherly tone.

The youth felt instant panic at this question. At first, he did not understand its full meaning.

"What?" he asked.

"Where you hit?" repeated the tattered man.

"Why," began the youth, "I—I—that is—why—I—"

He turned away suddenly and slid through the crowd. His brow was heavily flushed. His fingers were picking nervously at one of his buttons. He bent his head and fastened his eyes steadily upon the button. He acted as if it were a little problem.

The tattered man looked after him in astonishment.

Chapter 9

Vocabulary Preview

Below is a list of words that appear in this chapter. Review the list and get to know the words before you read the chapter.

enveloped surrounded; enclosed
envious jealous
hysterically wildly; madly
plight condition; situation
rendezvous meeting place
wrench twist; yank

The youth fell back in the procession until the tattered soldier was not in sight. Then he started to walk on with the others.

But he was amid wounds. The mob of men was bleeding. Because of the tattered soldier's questions, he now felt that his shame could be viewed. He was continually casting sidelong glances at the other men. He tried to see if they were noticing the letters of guilt he felt burned into his brow.

At times he regarded the wounded soldiers in an **envious** way. He thought that persons with wounds were curiously happy. He wished that he, too, had a wound, a red badge of courage.

The ghostly soldier was at his side like shadowing disgrace. The man's eyes were still fixed in a stare into the unknown. His gray, frightful face had attracted attention in the crowd. Men slowed to his dreary pace and walked with him.

They were discussing his **plight.** They questioned him and gave him advice. In a dogged way, he rejected them. He signed to them to go on and leave him alone.

The shadows of his face were deepening. His tight lips seemed holding in check the moan of great despair. There could be seen a certain stiffness in the movements of his body. It was as if he were taking great care not to arouse the passion of his wounds.

As he went on, he seemed always looking for a place. He was like one who goes to choose a grave.

The man continued to wave the bloody and pitying soldiers away. Something in the gesture made the youth start as if bitten. He yelled in horror. Tottering forward, he laid a quivering hand upon the man's arm. The soldier slowly turned his waxlike features toward him. The youth screamed.

"God! Jim Conklin!"

The tall soldier made a little ordinary smile. "Hello, Henry," he said.

The youth swayed on his legs and glared strangely. He stuttered and stammered. "Oh, Jim—oh, Jim—oh, Jim—"

The tall soldier held out his gory hand. There was a curious red and black combination of new blood and old blood upon it.

"Where you been, Henry?" he asked. He continued in a dull voice, "I thought maybe you got keeled over. There's been thunder to pay today. I was worryin' about it a good deal."

The youth still cried sadly. "Oh, Jim—oh, Jim—oh, Jim—"

"You know," said the tall soldier, "I was out there." He made a careful gesture. "And, Lord, what a circus! And, by jiminey, I got shot—I got shot. Yes, by jiminey, I got shot." He repeated this fact in a confused way. It was as if he did not know how it came about.

The youth put forth anxious arms to assist him. But the tall soldier went firmly on as if propelled. Since the youth's arrival as a guardian for his friend, the other wounded men had stopped showing much interest. They busied themselves again in dragging their own tragedies toward the rear.

The two friends marched on. Suddenly, the tall soldier

seemed to be overcome by a terror. His face took the appearance of gray paste. He clutched the youth's arm and looked all about him. It was as if he dreaded to be overheard. Then he began to speak in a shaking whisper.

"I tell you what I'm afraid of, Henry—I'll tell you what I'm afraid of. I'm afraid I'll fall down. And then you know—them damned artillery wagons—they like as not will run over me. That's what I'm afraid of—"

The youth cried out to him **hysterically**, "I'll take care of you, Jim! I'll take care of you! I swear to God I will!"

"Sure—will you, Henry?" the tall soldier begged.

"Yes—yes—I tell you—I'll take care of you, Jim!" declared the youth. He could not speak accurately because of the gulping in his throat.

But the tall soldier continued to beg in a humble way. He now hung babelike to the youth's arm. His eyes rolled in the wildness of his terror.

"I was always a good friend to you, wasn't I, Henry? I've always been a pretty good feller, ain't I? And it ain't much to ask, is it? Just to pull me along out of the road? I'd do it for you, wouldn't I, Henry?"

He paused in heartbreaking worry, waiting for his friend's reply.

The youth had reached a point of pain where the sobs scorched him. He tried to express his loyalty. But he could only make fantastic gestures.

However, the tall soldier seemed suddenly to forget all those fears. He became again the grim, stalking ghost of a soldier. He went stonily forward.

The youth wished his friend to lean upon him. But the other always shook his head and strangely protested.

"No—no—no—leave me be—leave me be—"

His look was fixed again upon the unknown. He moved with mysterious purpose. He brushed aside all of the youth's offers.

"No—no—leave me be—leave me be—"

The youth had to follow.

Soon, the youth heard a voice talking softly near his shoulders. Turning, he saw that it belonged to the tattered soldier.

"You'd better take him out of the road, partner. There's a battery comin' like a bat out of hell down the road. He'll get runned over. He's a goner anyhow in about five minutes. You can see that. You'd better take him out of the road. Where the blazes does he get his strength from?"

"Lord knows!" cried the youth. He was shaking his hands helplessly.

Soon, he ran forward and grasped the tall soldier by the arm. "Jim! Jim!" he coaxed. "Come with me."

The tall soldier weakly tried to **wrench** himself free. "Huh," he said emptily. He stared at the youth for a moment. At last he spoke as if dimly understanding. "Oh! Into the fields? Oh!"

He started blindly through the grass.

The youth turned once to look at the lashing riders and bouncing guns of the battery. He was startled from this view by a shrill outcry from the tattered man.

"God! He's runnin'!"

The youth turned his head swiftly. He saw his friend running in a staggering and stumbling way toward a little clump of bushes. The youth's heart seemed to wrench itself almost free from his body at this sight. He made a noise of pain. He and the tattered man began a pursuit. There was a singular race.

The youth overtook the tall soldier. Then he began to plead with all the words he could find. "Jim—Jim—what are you doing—what makes you do this way—you'll hurt yourself."

The same purpose was in the tall soldier's face. He protested in a dulled way. He kept his eyes fastened on the secret place of his thoughts. "No—no," he said. "Don't touch me—leave me be—leave me be—"

The youth was filled with horror and wonder at the tall soldier. Hesitating, he began to question him. "Where you goin', Jim? What you thinkin' about? Where you goin'? Tell me, won't you, Jim?"

The tall soldier turned around. He looked as if he were being chased without mercy. His eyes begged. "Leave me be, can't you? Leave me be for a minute.''

The youth drew back. "Why, Jim," he said, in a dazed way, "what's the matter with you?"

The tall soldier turned, staggered dangerously, and went on. The youth and the tattered soldier followed, sneaking as if whipped. They felt unable to face the stricken man if he should again face them.

They began to have thoughts of a solemn ceremony. The doomed soldier's movements were like a performance. And there was a resemblance in him to a follower of a mad religion—blood-sucking, muscle-wrenching, bone-crushing. They were awed and afraid. They hung back in case he had at command a dreadful weapon.

At last, they saw him stop and stand motionless. They hurried, then saw the expression on his face. It told them that he had at last found the place for which he had struggled.

His skinny figure was upright. His bloody hands were quietly at his side. He was waiting with patience for something that he had come to meet. He was at the **rendez-vous.** They paused and stood, waiting.

There was a silence.

Finally, the chest of the doomed soldier began to heave with a strained motion. It increased in violence. It was as if an animal was within and was kicking and tumbling madly to be free.

This sight of gradual choking made the youth twist about. The tall soldier rolled his eyes. And the youth saw something in them that made him sink wailing to the ground. He raised his voice in a last supreme call.

"Jim—Jim—Jim—"

The tall soldier opened his lips and spoke. He made a gesture. "Leave me be—don't touch me—leave me be—"

There was another silence while he waited.

Suddenly, his form stiffened and straightened. Then it was shaken by a prolonged fever. He stared into space. The two watchers observed the firm lines of his awful face. They saw a curious and moving dignity there.

He was invaded by a creeping strangeness that slowly

enveloped him. For a moment a trembling came to his legs. It caused him to dance a sort of hideous hornpipe.[1] His arms beat wildly about his head in expression of demonlike enthusiasm.

His tall figure stretched itself to its full height. There was a slight tearing sound. Then it began to swing forward, slow and straight, in the manner of a falling tree. A swift muscular twist made the left shoulder strike the ground first.

The body seemed to bounce a little way from the earth. "God!" said the tattered soldier.

The youth had watched, spellbound, this ceremony at the place of meeting. His face had been twisted into an expression of every pain he had imagined for his friend.

He now sprang to his feet. Going closer, he gazed upon the pastelike face. The mouth was open and the teeth showed in a laugh.

The flap of the blue jacket fell away from the body. He could see that the side looked as if it had been chewed by wolves.

The youth turned with sudden, wild rage toward the battlefield. He shook his fist. He seemed about to deliver a bitter insult.

"Hell—"

The red sun was pasted in the sky like a wafer.

[1]The hornpipe is a lively British folk dance.

Chapter 10 (Summary)

The tattered man stood over the dead soldier. He spoke in amazement of the strange death he and the youth had just witnessed. But the youth's grief kept him from responding.

Soon the youth's attention was drawn to the poor condition of the tattered man. He realized that the man was gravely injured and begged him not to die too.

But the tattered man seemed more worried about the youth than himself. He began to ask the youth about his wounds. The man's questions tore at the youth's conscience. He lashed out at the tattered man and told him he didn't want to be bothered.

The youth's shame at faking a wound plagued him until he could stand it no more. He was determined that the tattered man not discover the truth. So after saying an abrupt good-bye, he turned and left. The injured man stood alone in the field, begging the youth not to leave him.

The youth's shame was so overpowering he wished he were dead. He felt sure his secret would be revealed. And he realized he did not have the power to prevent it from happening.

Chapter 11

Vocabulary Preview

Below is a list of words that appear in this chapter.
Review the list and get to know the words before
you read the chapter.

calamity misery; disaster
exhortations pep talks; urgings
forlorn miserable; sad
frenzy wild excitement
valiant brave; fearless
vindication proof of innocence; removal of guilt

He became aware that the furnace roar of the battle was
growing louder. Great brown clouds had floated to the still
heights of the air before him. The noise, too, was approaching. The woods filtered men and the fields became
dotted.

As he rounded a small hill, he saw that the roadway was
now a crying mass of wagons, teams, and men. From the
heaving tangle issued **exhortations,** commands, and curses.
Fear was sweeping it all along.

The cracking whips bit and horses plunged and tugged.
The white-topped wagons strained and stumbled in their
struggles like fat sheep.

The youth felt comforted in a measure by this sight. They
were all retreating. Perhaps, then, he was not so bad after
all. He seated himself and watched the terror-stricken
wagons. They fled like soft, clumsy animals.

All the roarers and lashers served to help him magnify

the dangers and horrors of the battle. Other men might accuse him of being a coward. But he tried to prove to himself that it was, in truth, what anybody would do. He felt some pleasure in watching the wild march of this **vindication.**

Soon, the calm head of a forward-going column of infantry appeared in the road. It came swiftly on. Avoiding the obstacles gave it the winding movement of a serpent.

The men at the head butted mules with their musket stocks. They prodded teamsters[1] unconcerned about all howls. The men forced their way through parts of the dense crowd by strength. The blunt head of the column pushed. The raving teamsters swore many strange oaths.

The commands to make way had the ring of great importance in them. The men were going forward to the heart of the noise. They were to confront the eager rush of the enemy. They felt the pride of their onward movement.

The remainder of the army seemed trying to dribble down this road. They tumbled teams about with a fine feeling that it was no matter, as long as their column got to the front in time. This importance made their faces grave and stern. And the backs of the officers were very straight.

As the youth looked at them, the black weight of his grief returned to him. He felt that he was looking at a march of chosen beings. The separation was great to him. It was as if they had marched with weapons of flame and banners of sunlight. He could never be like them. He could have wept in his longings.

He searched about in his mind for a strong enough curse for whatever had caused this. Men always turn their words of final blame on some such thing. It—whatever it was— was responsible for him, he said. There lay the fault.

The column was in great haste to reach the battle. This seemed to the **forlorn** young man to be something much finer than hard fighting. Heroes, he thought, could find excuses in that long, angry line. They could retire with perfect self-respect and make excuses to the stars.

---

[1]A teamster drives a team of horses pulling a wagon.

He wondered what those men had eaten that they could be in such haste to force their way to grim chances of death. As he watched, his envy grew until he thought that he wished to change lives with one of them. He would have liked to have used a mighty force, he said, and throw off himself and become a better.

Swift pictures of himself, apart, yet in himself, came to him. He was a blue, desperate figure, leading wild charges. He held one knee forward and a broken blade high.

He was a blue, determined figure, standing before a red and steel attack. He would get calmly killed on a high place before the eyes of all. He thought of the splendid sorrow of his dead body.

These thoughts uplifted him. He felt the trembling of war desire. In his ears, he heard the ring of victory. He knew the **frenzy** of a rapid successful charge.

He heard the music of the trampling feet, the sharp voices, the clanking arms of the column near him. They made him soar on the red wings of war. For a few moments he was sublime.

He thought that he was about to start for the front. Indeed, he saw just such a picture of himself. He was dust-stained, wild-looking, and panting. He was flying to the front at the proper moment. He was about to seize and choke the dark, grinning witch of **calamity.**

Then the difficulties of the thing began to drag at him. He hesitated, balancing awkwardly on one foot.

He had no rifle. He could not fight with his hands, said he resentfully to his plan. Well, rifles could be had for the picking. They were very plentiful.

Also, he continued, it would be a miracle if he found his regiment. Well, he could fight with any regiment.

He started forward slowly. He stepped as if he expected to tread upon some explosive thing. Doubts and he were struggling.

He would truly be a worm if any of his comrades should see him returning thus. He had the marks of his flight upon him. There was a reply that serious fighters did not care for what happened rearward except that no hostile bayonets[2] appeared there.

In the blur of the battle, his face would, in a way, be hidden. It would be like the face of a hooded man.

But then he thought of something else his tireless fate would bring forth. When the battle slowed for a moment, a man would ask him for an explanation. In imagination, he felt the watching eyes of his companions as he painfully struggled through some lies.

Eventually, his courage wore itself out in these objections. The debates drained him of his fire.

He was not cast down by this defeat of his plan. For, upon studying the affair carefully, he could not but admit that the objections were very strong.

Furthermore, various hurts had begun to cry out. In their presence, he could not continue in flying high with the wings of war. They made it almost impossible for him to see himself in a heroic light. He tumbled headlong.

He discovered that he had a scorching thirst. His face was so dry and grimy that he thought he could feel his skin crackle. Each bone of his body had an ache in it. His body seemed to threaten to break with each movement.

His feet were like two sores. Also, his body was calling for food. It was more powerful than a direct hunger. There was a dull, weightlike feeling in his stomach. When he tried to walk, his head swayed and he tottered.

He could not see very clearly. Small patches of green mist floated before his vision.

While he had been tossed by many emotions, he had not been aware of his pains. Now they attacked him and cried out. At last he was forced to pay attention to them. And so his ability for self-hate was multiplied.

In despair, he declared that he was not like those others. He now confessed it to be impossible that he should ever become a hero. He was a cowardly fool.

Those pictures of glory were sad things. He groaned from

[2]Bayonets are sharp blades attached to the ends of rifles. They are used in hand-to-hand combat.

his heart and went staggering off.

A certain mothlike quality within him kept him in the area of the battle. He had a great desire to see, and to get news. He wished to know who was winning.

He told himself that, despite his enormous suffering, he had never lost his greed for victory. Yet, he spoke in a half-apologetic manner to his conscience. He could not but know that a defeat for the army this time might mean many favorable things to him.

The blows of the enemy would splinter regiments into pieces. Thus, many men of courage, he thought, would be forced to desert the colors and scurry like chickens.

He would appear as one of them. They would be gloomy brothers in distress. He could then easily believe he had not run any farther or faster than they. And if he himself could believe in his fine perfection, he felt there would be small trouble in convincing all others.

He made excuses for this hope. He said that the army had met great defeats before. But in a few months, it had shaken off all blood and sign of them. It came back as bright and **valiant** as a new one.

The army had thrust out of sight the memory of disaster. It appeared with the courage and confidence of unconquered troops. The noisy voices of the people at home would sound cheerless for a time. But various generals usually had to listen to these little songs.

He, of course, felt no regrets about proposing a general as a sacrifice. He could not tell who might be chosen for the insults. So he could give him no direct sympathy.

The people were far off, and he did not think public opinion would be accurate at long range. It was quite likely they would hit the wrong man. First, he would have to recover from his amazement. Then he would spend the rest of his days in writing replies to the songs of his supposed failure.

It would be very unfortunate, no doubt. But in this case, a general was of no concern to the youth.

In a defeat, there would be a roundabout vindication of himself. He thought it would prove, in a way, that he had fled early because he had a special way of seeing things. A serious prophet, upon predicting a flood, should be the first man to climb a tree. This showed that he was, indeed, a seer.[3]

A moral vindication was regarded by the youth as a very important thing. Without it he could not, he thought, wear the sore badge of his dishonor through life. He needed something to soothe his wound.

His heart was continually telling him that he was worthless. He could not exist without making it, through his actions, public to all men.

If the army had gone gloriously on, he would be lost. If the noise meant that now his army's flags were tilted forward, he was a condemned wretch. He would be forced to doom himself to isolation. If the men were advancing, their unconcerned feet were trampling upon his chances for a successful life.

These thoughts went quickly through his mind. He turned upon them and tried to thrust them away. He condemned himself as a villain. He said that he was the most thoroughly selfish man alive.

His mind pictured soldiers who would place their bold bodies before the spear of the yelling enemy. He saw their dripping corpses on an imagined field. He said that he was their murderer.

Again, he thought that he wished he was dead. He believed that he envied a corpse. Thinking of the slain, he felt a great contempt for some of them. It was as if they were guilty for thus becoming lifeless.

They might have been killed by lucky chances, he said. They might have died before they had a chance to flee, or before they had been really tested. Yet they would receive all the usual honors.

He cried out bitterly that their crowns were stolen. Their robes of glorious memories were fakes. However, he still said it was a great pity he was not as they.

He wished for the defeat of the army. It seemed to him a means of escape from the outcome of his fall. He thought

[3]A prophet, or seer, can see the future and predict what will happen.

now, however, that it was useless to think of such a chance.

All he knew told him that success for that mighty blue machine was certain. It would make victories as a factory turns out buttons. He soon gave up thinking otherwise. He returned to the belief of soldiers.

So now he saw again that it was not possible for the army to be defeated. He tried to think up a fine tale which he could take back to his regiment. He needed one to turn away the expected laughter.

But as much as he feared this laughter, it became impossible for him to invent a tale he felt he could trust. He experimented with many plans. He threw them aside one by one as flimsy. He was quick to see weak places in them all.

Furthermore, he was much afraid that some arrow of laughter would catch him off guard. And he might not have a chance to raise his protecting tale.

He imagined the whole regiment saying, "Where's Henry Fleming? He run, didn't he? Oh, my!"

He recalled certain persons who would be quite sure to leave him no peace about it. They would doubtless question him with sneers. They would laugh at his stammering hesitation. In the next battle, they would try to keep watch of him closely to discover when he would run.

Wherever he went in camp, he would meet bold and drawn-out stares of cruelty. As he imagined himself passing near a crowd of comrades, he could hear some one say, "There he goes!"

Then, as if the heads were moved by one muscle, all the faces were turned toward him with wide, mocking grins. He seemed to hear some one make a humorous remark in a low tone. The others all crowed and cackled at it. He was a slang phrase.[4]

---

[4]Slang is informal speech used by a particular group or culture. In slang, a name often becomes a term for a certain type of person (*scrooge* means "a stingy, cranky person"). Crane means that Henry's name would be used by his fellow soldiers to mean "coward."

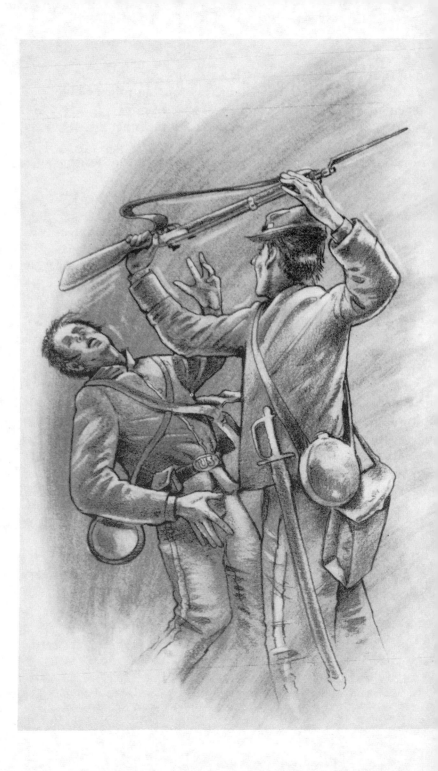

Chapter 12

Vocabulary Preview

Below is a list of words that appear in this chapter. Review the list and get to know the words before you read the chapter.

anticipation expectation
balking unwilling; hesitating
incoherent confused; mixed-up
philosophy theory; viewpoint
somber dark; gloomy
writhing twisting; thrashing about

The column had been butting fearlessly at the obstacles in the roadway. It was barely out of the youth's sight before he saw dark waves of men. They came sweeping out of the woods and down through the fields.

He knew at once that the steel fibers had been washed from their hearts. They were bursting from their coats and their equipments as from prisons. They charged down upon him like terrified buffaloes.

Behind them, blue smoke curled and clouded above the treetops. Through the thickets, he could sometimes see a distinct pink glare. The voices of the cannon were crying out in an endless chorus.

The youth was struck with horror. He stared in pain and amazement. He forgot that he was engaged in fighting the universe. He threw aside his mental pamphlets on the **philosophy** of the retreated and the rules for the guidance of the damned.

The fight was lost. The dragons were coming with mighty

strides. The army was helpless in the matted thickets and blinded by the overhanging night. It was going to be swallowed. War, the red animal, war, the blood-swollen god, would have its bloated fill.

Within him, something wanted to cry out. He had the impulse to make a rallying speech, to sing a battle hymn. But he could only get his tongue to call into the air, "Why—why—what—what's the matter?"

Soon he was in the midst of them. They were leaping and scampering all about him. Their pale faces shone in the dusk. They seemed, for the most part, to be very burly men.

The youth turned from one to another of them as they galloped along. His **incoherent** questions were lost. They paid no attention to his appeals. They did not seem to see him.

They sometimes chattered madly. One huge man was asking the sky, "Say, where's the plank road? Where's the plank road!" It was as if he had lost a child. The man wept in his pain and dismay.

Soon, men were running here and there in all ways. The artillery boomed, forward and rearward. On the sides, it made a jumble of ideas of direction. Landmarks had vanished into the gathering gloom.

The youth began to imagine that he had got into the center of the terrible quarrel. He could see no way out of it. From the mouths of the fleeing men came a thousand wild questions. No one made answers.

The youth rushed about, throwing questions at the unhearing bands of retreating infantry. Finally, he clutched a man by the arm. They swung around face to face.

"Why—why—" stammered the youth, struggling with his **balking** tongue.

The man screamed, "Let go me! Let go me!"

His face was pale and his eyes were rolling uncontrolled. He was heaving and panting. He still grasped his rifle. Perhaps he had forgotten to release his hold upon it.

The man tugged frantically. The youth was forced to lean forward and was dragged several paces.

"Let go me! Let go me!"

"Why—why—" stuttered the youth.

"Well, then!" bawled the man in a wild rage. He quickly and fiercely swung his rifle. It crushed upon the youth's
head. The man ran on.

The youth's fingers had turned to paste upon the other's
arm. The energy vanished from his muscles. He saw the
flaming wings of lightning flash before his vision. There was
a deafening rumble of thunder within his head.

Suddenly his legs seemed to die. He sank **writhing** to the
ground. He tried to arise. In his efforts against the numb-
ing pain, he was like a man wrestling with a creature of the
air.

There was a fierce struggle. Sometimes he would get
halfway to his feet. He would battle with the air for a moment. Then he would fall again, grabbing at the grass. His
face was a damp paleness. Deep groans were wrenched from
him.

At last, with a twisting movement, he got upon his hands
and knees. From there he got to his feet, like a babe trying
to walk. Pressing his hands to his temples, he went staggering over the grass.

He fought an intense battle with his body. His dulled
senses wished him to faint. He opposed them stubbornly.
His mind pictured unknown dangers and injuries if he should
fall upon the field.

He went tall soldier fashion. He imagined lonely spots
where he could fall and be left alone. To search for one,
he fought against the tide of his pain.

Once he put his hand to the top of his head and carefully
touched the wound. He felt a scratching pain at the contact. It made him draw a long breath through his clinched
teeth. His fingers were dabbled with blood. He looked at
them with a fixed stare.

Around him, he could hear the grumble of jolted cannon. Scurrying horses were being lashed toward the front.
Once, a young officer on a charger nearly ran him down.

He turned and watched the mass of guns, men, and
horses. They were sweeping in a wide curve toward a gap
in a fence. The officer was making excited motions with a

gloved hand. The guns followed the teams with an air of unwillingness. It was as if they were being dragged by the heels.

Some officers of the scattered infantry were cursing and yelling like fishwives.[1] Their scolding voices could be heard above the noise. Into the unspeakable jumble in the roadway rode a squadron of cavalry.[2] The faded yellow of the trimming on their uniforms shone bravely. There was a mighty quarrel.

The artillery was gathering as if for a meeting.

The blue haze of evening was upon the field. The lines of forest were long purple shadows. One cloud lay along the western sky, partly smothering the red.

The youth left the scene behind him. Then he heard the guns suddenly roar out. He imagined them shaking in black rage. They belched and howled like brass devils guarding a gate. The soft air was filled with the mighty protest. With it came the shattering ring of opposing infantry.

The youth turned to look behind him. He could see sheets of orange light brighten up the shadowy distance. There were subtle and sudden lightnings in the far air. At times he thought he could see heaving masses of men.

He hurried on in the dusk. The day had faded until he could barely see the way for his feet. The purple darkness was filled with men who lectured and jabbered. Sometimes he could see them gesturing against the blue and **somber** sky. There seemed to be a great number of men and weapons spread about in the forest and in the fields.

The little narrow roadway now lay lifeless. There were overturned wagons like sun-dried boulders. Before, the road had been like a riverbed to the rushing army. Now it was choked with the bodies of horses and splintered parts of war machines.

It had come to pass that his wound pained him but little. He was afraid to move quickly, however, for dread of disturbing it. He held his head very still and took much care

[1] A fishwife is a shrew—a loud, scolding woman.
[2] A squadron is smaller than a company. (See the military chart on page 146.) In a cavalry unit, soldiers ride on horseback.

against stumbling.

He was filled with anxiety. His face was pinched and drawn in **anticipation** of the pain of any sudden mistake of his feet in the gloom.

His thoughts, as he walked, fixed carefully upon his hurt. There was a cool, liquid feeling about it. He imagined blood moving slowly down under his hair. His head seemed swollen to a size that made him think his neck was too small.

The new silence of his wound made him worry. Before, he had heard little blistering voices of pain calling out from his scalp. He had thought they were clear in their expression of danger. By them, he believed he could measure his distress.

But now they were dangerously silent. So he became frightened. He imagined terrible fingers that clutched into his brain.

Amid it, he began to remember different events and conditions of the past. He thought about certain meals his mother had cooked at home. He especially remembered meals that included food he was particularly fond of. He saw the spread table. The pine walls of the kitchen were glowing in the warm light from the stove.

Too, he remembered how he and his friends used to go from the schoolhouse to the bank of a shaded pool. He saw his clothes in a disorderly pile upon the grass of the bank. He felt the swash of the fragrant water upon his body. The leaves of the overhanging maple rustled. There was a melody in the wind of youthful summer.

He was soon overcome by a dragging weariness. His head hung forward and his shoulders were stooped. It was as if he were carrying a great bundle. His feet shuffled along the ground.

He held continuous arguments with himself. Should he lie down and sleep at some near spot? Or should he force himself on until he reached a safe place?

He often tried to dismiss these questions, but his body kept rebelling. His senses nagged at him like spoiled babies.

At last, he heard a cheery voice near his shoulder. "You seem to be in a pretty bad way, boy?"

The youth did not look up, but he agreed with thick tongue. "Uh!"

The owner of the cheery voice took him firmly by the arm. "Well," he said, with a round laugh, "I'm goin' your way. The whole gang is goin' your way. And I guess I can give you a lift." They began to walk like a drunken man and his friend.

As they went along, the man questioned the youth. He helped him with the replies like someone coaxing the mind of a child. Sometimes he threw in little stories.

"What regiment do you belong to? Eh? What's that? The 304th New York? Why, what corps is that in? Oh, it is? Why, I thought they wasn't fightin' today. They're way over in the center.

"Oh, they was, eh? Well, pretty nearly everybody got their share of fightin' today. By dad, I give myself up for dead any number of times.

"There was shootin' here and shootin' there, and hollerin' here and hollerin' there. It was all in the damned darkness. I couldn't tell to save my soul which side I was on.

"Sometimes I thought I was sure enough from Ohio. And other times I could have swore I was from the bitter end of Florida. It was the most mixed up dern thing I ever see.

"And these here whole woods is a regular mess. It'll be a miracle if we find our regiments tonight. Pretty soon, though, we'll meet plenty of guards and military police, and one thing and another.

"Ho! There they go with an officer, I guess. Look at his hand a-draggin'. He's got all the war he wants, I bet. He won't be talkin' so big about his reputation and all when they go to sawin' off his leg. Poor feller! My brother's got whiskers just like that. How did you get 'way over here, anyhow? Your regiment is a long way from here, ain't it? Well, I guess we can find it.

"You know, there was a boy killed in my company today. I thought the world and all of him. Jack was a nice feller. By ginger, it hurt like thunder to see ol' Jack just get knocked flat.

"We was a-standin' pretty peaceable for a spell. There

was men runnin' every way all around us, though. And while we was a-standin' like that, along comes a big fat feller. He began to peck at Jack's elbow. He says, 'Say, where's the road to the river?'

"And Jack, he never paid no attention. And the feller kept on a-peckin' at his elbow and sayin', 'Say, where's the road to the river?'

"Jack was a-lookin' ahead all the time. He was tryin' to see the Johnnies comin' through the woods. He never paid no attention to this big fat feller for a long time. But at last he turned around and he says, 'Ah, go to hell and find the road to the river!'

"And just then, a shot slapped him bang on the side of the head. He was a sergeant, too. Them was his last words.

"Thunder, I wish we was sure of findin' our regiments tonight. It's goin' to be long huntin'. But I guess we can do it."

In the search that followed, the man of the cheery voice seemed to the youth to possess a wand of a magic kind. He threaded the mazes of the tangled forest with a strange fortune.

They met guards and patrols. But he showed the sharpness of a detective and the boldness of a homeless child. Obstacles fell before him and became of help.

The youth's chin was still on his breast. He stood woodenly by while his companion beat ways and means out of difficult things.

The forest seemed a vast hive of men buzzing about in frantic circles. But the cheery man led the youth without mistakes. At last he began to chuckle with glee and self-satisfaction. "Ah, there you are! See that fire?"

The youth nodded stupidly.

"Well, there's where your regiment is. And now, good-by, ol' boy. Good luck to you."

A warm and strong hand clasped the youth's weak fingers for an instant. Then he heard a cheerful and brave whistling as the man walked away. He who had so befriended him was now passing out of his life. It suddenly occurred to the youth that he had not once seen his face.

Chapter 13 (Summary)

The youth wanted to go off deeper into the darkness and hide. But his pain and fatigue forced him to move toward the fire.

Before he reached it, he was halted by the soldier on guard. The youth was relieved to see it was his friend Wilson. The loud soldier asked what had happened to the youth.

Hurriedly Henry came up with a tale to explain his wound. He claimed he had been shot in the head after being separated from the regiment.

The corporal appeared and led the youth over to the fire. He inspected the youth's wound and was satisfied that it wasn't too serious. He went to get Wilson, who would take care of the wound.

The youth surveyed the sleeping soldiers. Their exhausted bodies cluttered the ground.

The loud soldier arrived, made a crude bandage out of a handkerchief, and bound it to the youth's head. As he worked, Wilson spoke of his admiration for Henry, and the youth became uncomfortable. Then the loud soldier gave his coat to the youth and made a bed for him to sleep on.

The youth drifted off to sleep listening to the sound of muskets in the distance. He wondered if the men firing them ever slept.

Chapter 14

When the youth awoke, it seemed to him that he had been asleep for a thousand years. He felt sure that he opened his eyes upon an unexpected world.

Gray mists were slowly shifting before the first efforts of the sun rays. A coming splendor could be seen in the eastern sky. An icy dew had chilled his face. Immediately upon waking, he curled farther down into his blanket.

He stared for a while at the leaves overhead. They moved in a messengerlike wind of the day.

The distance was shattering and blaring with the noise of fighting. There was in the sound an expression of deadly determination. It was as if it had not begun and was not going to stop.

About him were the rows and groups of men that he had dimly seen the night before. They were getting a last taste of sleep before the awakening.

The grim, tired faces and dusty figures were made plain by this odd light at the dawning. But it dressed the skin of the men in corpselike colors. It made the tangled limbs appear pulseless and dead.

The youth started up with a little cry when his eyes first swept over this motionless mass of men. They were thick-spread upon the ground, pale, and in strange postures.

His disordered mind thought the hall of the forest to be a cemetery. He believed for an instant that he was in the house of the dead. He did not dare to move, lest these corpses start up, squalling and squawking.

In a second, however, he achieved his proper mind. He swore a complicated oath at himself. He saw that this somber picture was not a fact of the present. It was a mere **prophecy.**

He then heard the noise of a fire crackling briskly in the cold air. Turning his head, he saw his friend puttering busily about a small blaze. A few other figures moved in the fog. He heard the hard cracking of axe blows.

Suddenly, there was a hollow rumble of drums. A distant bugle sang faintly. Similar sounds, varying in strength, came from near and far over the forest.

The bugles called to each other like noisy roosters. The near thunder of the regimental drums rolled.

The body of men in the woods rustled. There was a general uplifting of heads. A murmuring of voices broke upon the air. In it, there was the low sound of grumbling oaths.

The voices addressed strange gods. They complained to them about the early hours necessary to correct war. An officer's high, commanding voice rang out. It quickened the stiffened movement of the men. The tangled limbs unraveled. The corpse-colored faces were hidden behind fists that twisted slowly in the eye sockets.

The youth sat up and let out an enormous yawn.

"Thunder!" he remarked complainingly. He rubbed his eyes. Then, putting up his hand, he felt carefully of the bandage over his wound. His friend saw that he was awake and came from the fire.

"Well, Henry, ol' man, how do you feel this mornin'?"

he demanded.

The youth yawned again. Then he puckered his mouth to a little pucker. His head, in truth, felt just like a melon. There was an unpleasant sensation in his stomach.

"Oh, Lord, I feel pretty bad," he said.

"Thunder!" exclaimed the other. "I hoped you'd feel all right this mornin'. Let's see the bandage. I guess it's slipped." He began to tinker at the wound in rather a clumsy way. At last, the youth exploded.

"Gosh-dern it!" he said in sharp irritation. "You're the hangdest man I ever saw! You wear muffs on your hands. Why in good thunderation can't you be more easy? I'd rather you'd stand off and throw guns at it. Now, go slow. Don't act as if you was nailin' down carpet."

The youth glared with **insolent** command at his friend. But the loud soldier answered soothingly. "Well, well, come now, and get some grub," he said. "Then, maybe, you'll feel better."

At the fireside, the loud young soldier watched over his comrade's wants with tenderness and care. He very busily gathered up the little black runaway tin cups. He poured into them the streaming, iron-colored mixture from a small and sooty tin pail.

He had some fresh meat which he roasted hurriedly upon a stick. He sat down then, and watched the youth's appetite with glee.

The youth took note of a remarkable change in his comrade. It had come since those days of camp life upon the river bank. He seemed no more to be always thinking about the size of his personal abilities. He was not furious at small words that pricked his pride. He was no more a loud young soldier.

There was about him now a fine trust. He showed a quiet belief in his purposes and his abilities. And this inward confidence seemed to give him strength. Now he could be **indifferent** to little words of other men aimed at him.

The youth looked back on things. He had been used to regarding his comrade as a **blatant** child. His boldness had seemed to grow from inexperience. He had been thoughtless, headstrong, jealous, and filled with a showy courage. He had been a prancing babe used to strutting in his own dooryard.

The youth wondered where these new eyes had been born. When had his comrade made this great discovery that there were many men who would refuse to put up with him?

Apparently, the other seemed to have now climbed to a peak of wisdom. From it, he could see himself as a very wee thing. And the youth saw that ever after it would be easier to live in his friend's neighborhood.

His comrade balanced his black coffee cup on his knee. "Well, Henry," he said, "what do you think the chances are? Do you think we'll wallop 'em?"

The youth considered for a moment. "Day-before-yesterday," he finally replied, with boldness, "you would have bet you'd lick the whole kit-and-boodle all by yourself."

His friend looked a trifle amazed. "Would I?" he asked. He thought. "Well, perhaps I would," he decided at last. He stared humbly at the fire.

The youth was quite disturbed at this surprising reception of his remarks. "Oh, no, you wouldn't either," he said, hastily trying to take it back.

But the other made a disapproving gesture. "Oh, you needn't mind, Henry," he said. "I believe I was a pretty big fool in those days." He spoke as if years had passed.

There was a little pause.

"All the officers say we've got the rebs in a pretty tight box," said the friend. He cleared his throat in an ordinary way. "They all seem to think we've got 'em just where we want 'em."

"I don't know about that," the youth replied. "What I seen over on the right makes me think it was the other way about. From where I was, it looked as if we was gettin' a good poundin' yesterday."

"Do you think so?" asked the friend. "I thought we handled 'em pretty rough yesterday."

"Not a bit," said the youth. "Why, lord, man, you didn't see nothing of the fight. Why!" Then a sudden thought came to him. "Oh! Jim Conklin's dead."

His friend started. "What? Is he? Jim Conklin?"

The youth spoke slowly. "Yes. He's dead. Shot in the side."

"You don't say so. Jim Conklin . . . poor cuss!"

All about them were other small fires. These were surrounded by men with their little black utensils. From one of these near came sudden sharp voices in a row.

It appeared that two light-footed soldiers had been teasing a huge, bearded man. They had caused him to spill coffee upon his blue knees. The man had gone into a rage and had sworn a great deal.

Stung by his language, his **tormentors** had immediately bristled at him. They made a great show of resenting his unjust oaths. Possibly there was going to be a fight.

The friend arose and went over to them. He made peaceful motions with his arms. "Oh, here, now, boys, what's the use?" he said. "We'll be at the rebs in less than an hour. What's the good fightin' among ourselves?"

One of the light-footed soldiers turned upon him. He was red-faced and violent. "You needn't come around here with your preachin'. I suppose you don't approve of fightin' since Charley Morgan licked you. But I don't see what business this here is of yours or anybody else."

"Well, it ain't," said the friend mildly. "Still, I hate to see—"

There was a tangled argument.

"Well, he—," said the two, pointing at their opponent with accusing forefingers.

The huge soldier was quite purple with rage. He pointed at the two soldiers with his great hand, held out clawlike. "Well, they—"

But during this argument, the desire to deal blows seemed to pass. They said much to each other, though. Finally, the friend returned to his old seat. In a short while, the three **antagonists** could be seen together in a friendly bunch.

"Jimmie Rogers says I'll have to fight him after the battle today," announced the friend as he again seated himself. "He says he don't allow no interferin' in his business. I hate to see the boys fightin' among themselves.''

The youth laughed. ''You changed a good bit. You ain't at all like you was. I remember when you and that Irish feller—'' He stopped and laughed again.

''No, I didn't use to be that way,'' said his friend thoughtfully. ''That's true enough.''

''Well, I didn't mean—'' began the youth.

The friend made another disapproving gesture. ''Oh, you needn't mind, Henry.''

There was another little pause.

''The regiment lost over half the men yesterday,'' remarked the friend eventually. ''I thought of course they was all dead. But, Lord, they kept a-comin' back last night. It seems after all we didn't lose but a few.

''They'd been scattered all over, wanderin' around in the woods. They'd been fightin' with other regiments, and everything. Just like you done.''

''So?'' said the youth.

Chapter 15

Vocabulary Preview

Below is a list of words that appear in this chapter. Review the list and get to know the words before you read the chapter.

condescension scornful or snobbish attitude
derision scorn; contempt
discretion caution; good judgment
impelled urged; driven
pompous vain; proud
retribution revenge; punishment

The regiment was standing at order arms[1] at the side of a lane. It was waiting for the command to march. Suddenly, the youth remembered the little packet wrapped in a faded yellow envelope. The loud young soldier had entrusted it to him with mournful words.

It made him start. He uttered an exclamation and turned toward his comrade.

"Wilson!"

"What?"

His friend was at his side in the ranks. He was thoughtfully staring down the road. For some cause, his expression was at that moment very meek. The youth, regarding him with sidelong glances, felt **impelled** to change his purpose. "Oh, nothin'," he said.

His friend turned his head in some surprise, "Why, what was you goin' to say?"

[1] When soldiers stand at order arms, they hold their rifles at their right with the rifle butts resting on the ground.

"Oh, nothin'," repeated the youth.

He decided not to deal the little blow. It was enough that the fact made him glad. It was not necessary to knock his friend on the head with the misguided packet.

He had been possessed of much fear of his friend. He saw how easily questions could make holes in his feelings.

Lately, he had assured himself that the changed comrade would not tempt him with a constant curiosity. But he worried about what would happen when the first chance arose. He felt certain that his friend would ask him to relate his adventures of the day before.

He now rejoiced in the possession of the small weapon. He could use it to lay his comrade low at the first signs of a cross-examination. He was master. It would now be he who could laugh and shoot the shafts of **derision.**

The friend had, in a weak hour, spoken with sobs of his own death. He had given a sad speech before his funeral. Doubtless the packet of letters included a number of keepsakes to relatives. But he had not died. Thus, he had delivered himself into the hands of the youth.

The youth felt greatly superior to his friend. But he was inclined to **condescension.** And he adopted toward him an air of scornful good humor.

The youth's self-pride was now entirely restored. In the shade of its rich growth, he stood with braced and self-confident legs. Nothing could now be held against him, so he did not shrink from a meeting with the eyes of judges.

He allowed no thoughts of his own to keep him from an attitude of manfulness. He had performed his mistakes in the dark, so he was still a man.

Now he remembered his fortunes of yesterday. And indeed, looking at them from a distance, he began to see something fine there. He had the right to be **pompous** and veteranlike.

His panting terrors of the past he put out of his sight. In the present, he declared something to himself. He decided it was only the doomed and the damned who roared with sincerity at circumstance.

A man with a full stomach and the respect of his fellow

had no business to scold about anything. What could he find wrong with the ways of the universe, or even with the ways of society? Let the unfortunates complain. The others may play marbles.

He did not give a great deal of thought to these battles that lay directly before him. It was not important that he should plan his ways in regard to them. He had been taught that many obligations of a life were easily avoided.

The lessons of yesterday had been that **retribution** was slow and blind. Now this seemed a fact to him. It did not seem necessary that he should become feverish over the possibilities of the coming twenty-four hours. He could leave much to chance.

Besides, a faith in himself had secretly blossomed. There was a little flower of confidence growing within him. He was now a man of experience.

He had been out among the dragons, he said. And he assured himself that they were not so ugly as he had imagined them. Also, they were inaccurate. They did not sting with great skill. A brave heart often dared, and, daring, escaped. And, furthermore, how could they kill him who was the chosen of gods and doomed to greatness?

He remembered how some of the men had run from the battle. As he recalled their terror-struck faces, he felt a scorn for them. They had surely been faster and wilder than was clearly necessary. They were weak mortals. As for himself, he had fled with **discretion** and dignity.

He was roused from these thoughts by his friend, who had hitched about nervously and blinked at the trees for a time. Now he coughed in an introductory way, and spoke.

"Fleming!"

"What?"

The friend put his hand up to his mouth and coughed again. He squirmed in his jacket.

"Well," he gulped, at last, "I guess you might as well give me back them letters." Dark, prickling blood had flushed into his cheeks and brow.

"All right, Wilson," said the youth. He loosened two buttons of his coat, thrust in his hand, and brought forth the packet. He extended it to his friend, whose face was turned from him.

The youth had been slow in the act of producing the packet because he had been trying to invent a remarkable comment upon the affair. He could come up with nothing that would make his point. He had to let his friend escape untroubled with his packet. And for this, he took unto himself great credit. It was a generous thing.

His friend at his side seemed to suffer great shame. As he watched him, the youth felt his heart grow more strong and determined. He had never felt the need to blush for his acts like this. He was an individual of unique virtues.

He thought, with humble pity, "Too bad! Too bad! The poor devil, it makes him feel tough!"

After this incident, he looked back on the battle pictures he had seen. He felt quite able to return home and make the hearts of the people glow with stories of war.

He could see himself in a room of warm tints, telling tales to listeners. He could show off his honors. They were without meaning. But in a place where honors were infrequent, they might shine.

He saw his gaping audience picturing him as the central figure in blazing scenes. And he imagined the amazement and outcries of his mother and the young lady at school as they drank his stories. They had had some vague feminine ideas of beloved ones doing brave deeds on the field of battle without risk. These ideas would be destroyed by his stories.

Chapter 16 (Summary)

The regiment marched toward some damp trenches in order to relieve a command. The soldiers could hear the dull popping of guns in the foggy woods beyond. The noise grew more steady as they drew nearer.

The fighting became more intense, and the men huddled behind a small hill. They awaited their turn to enter the battle.

Rumors spread like fire during their wait. The men criticized the uncertainty of their commanding officers and shared tales of defeat. They felt discouraged. In their opinion, they had fought courageously but did not have a victory to show for it.

At last the guns stopped, and the regiment moved on. The youth continued to express his anger. He loudly condemned the ranking officers. He tried to stop himself, but he only spoke more forcefully. He concluded that the losses were the officers' fault since the men had been fighting like the devil.

At this last remark, the youth grew silent with guilt. But when no one challenged the statement, he continued his verbal attacks.

Finally, a soldier grew annoyed with the youth and asked him if he had fought the last battle single-handedly. Embarrassed and threatened by the question, the youth again grew silent.

The regiment was halted once more. The men cursed the nearness of the gunfire. Behind them, the battery opened fire. The fight had begun once more. But this time the regiment hesitated. They stood together, waiting for the shock to hit them.

Chapter 17

Vocabulary Preview

Below is a list of words that appear in this chapter.
Review the list and get to know the words before
you read the chapter.

incomprehensible jumbled; beyond understanding
intent firm; determined
leisure spare time; time of rest
ruthless pitiless; heartless
surged rushed; flowed
vengeance revenge

This advance of the enemy seemed to the youth like a
ruthless hunting. He began to fume with rage and frustration. He beat his foot upon the ground. He scowled with
hate at the swirling smoke that was approaching like an
imaginary flood.

There was a maddening quality in this seeming determination of the foe to give him no rest or time to sit down and
think. Yesterday he had fought and had fled rapidly. There
had been many adventures. For today, he felt he had earned
the chance to sit and think.

He could have enjoyed talking to uninformed listeners.
He could have told them of various scenes at which he had
been a witness. Or he could ably discuss the processes of
war with other proved men.

It was also important that he should have time for physical
recovery. He was sore and stiff from his experiences. He
had received his fill of all struggles, and he wished to rest.

But those other men seemed never to grow weary. They were fighting with their old speed.

He had a wild hate for the tireless foe. Yesterday, he had imagined the universe to be against him. He had hated it, little gods and big gods. Today, he hated the army of the foe with the same great hatred.

He was not going to be badgered all his life, like a kitten chased by boys, he said. It was not well to drive men into final corners. At those moments, they could all develop teeth and claws.

He leaned and spoke into his friend's ear. He growled the words with a gesture. "If they keep on chasin' us, by God, they'd better watch out. Can't stand *too* much."

The friend twisted his head and made a calm reply.

"If they keep on a-chasin' us, they'll drive us all into the river."

The youth cried out savagely at this statement. He crouched behind a little tree. His eyes burned hatefully, and his teeth were set in a doglike snarl.

The awkward bandage was still about his head. Upon it, over his wound, there was a spot of dry blood. His hair was wondrously rumpled. Some straggling, moving locks of hair hung over the cloth of the bandage down toward his forehead.

His jacket and shirt were open at the throat and exposed his young, bronzed neck. There could be seen sudden gulpings at his throat.

His fingers twined nervously about his rifle. He wished that it was an engine of deathly power. He felt that he and his companions were being teased and made fun of. The enemy seemed to sincerely believe that they were poor and puny.

He knew too well his inability to take **vengeance** for it. This made his rage into a dark and stormy ghost. It possessed him and made him dream of hateful cruelties.

The tormentors were flies sucking disrespectfully at his blood. He thought he would have given his life for revenge. He wanted to see their faces in pitiful plights.

The winds of battle had swept all about the regiment. The

one rifle, instantly followed by others, flashed in its front. A moment later, the regiment roared forth its sudden and valiant reply.

A dense wall of smoke settled slowly down. It was furiously slit and slashed by the knifelike fire from the rifles.

To the youth, the fighters resembled animals. They had been tossed for a death struggle into a dark pit. There was a sensation that he and his fellows were at bay. They were pushing back, always pushing fierce attacks of creatures who were slippery.

Their red rifle shots seemed to have no effect upon the bodies of their foes. The enemy seemed to avoid them with ease. They came through, between, around, and about with unopposed skill.

In a dream, it occurred to the youth that his rifle was a useless stick. He then lost sense of everything but his hate. He wanted to smash into pulp the glittering smile of victory which he could feel upon the faces of his enemies.

The blue, smoke-swallowed line curled and writhed. It was like a snake that had been stepped upon. It swung its ends to and fro in a pain of fear and rage.

The youth was not aware that he was standing upon his feet. He did not know the direction of the ground. Indeed, once he even lost the habit of balance and fell heavily. He was up again immediately.

One thought went through the chaos of his brain at the time. He wondered if he had fallen because he had been shot. But the suspicion flew away at once. He did not think more of it.

He had taken up a first position behind the little tree. He had a direct determination to hold it against the world. He had not considered it possible that his army could that day succeed. From this, he felt the ability to fight harder.

But the crowd had **surged** in all ways. At last, he lost directions and locations. He only knew where lay the enemy.

The flames bit him, and the hot smoke broiled his skin. His rifle barrel grew so hot that ordinarily he could not have held it upon his palms. But he kept on stuffing cartridges into it. He pounded them with his clanking, bending ramrod.

If he aimed at some changing form through the smoke, he pulled his trigger with a fierce grunt. It was as if he were dealing a blow of the fist with all his strength.

Then the enemy seemed to fall back before him and his fellows. He went instantly forward. He was like a dog who, seeing his foes lagging behind, turns and insists upon being pursued. When he was forced to fall back again, he did it slowly, sullenly. He took steps of wrathful despair.

Once he, in his **intent** hate, was almost alone. He was firing when all those near him had ceased. He was so caught up in his occupation that he was not aware of a lull.

He was stopped by a hoarse laugh. A sentence came to his ears in a voice of contempt and amazement. "You infernal fool. Don't you know enough to quit when there ain't anything to shoot at? Good God!"

The youth turned then. He paused with his rifle thrown half into position. He looked at the blue line of his comrades. During this moment of **leisure,** they all seemed to be caught up in staring with astonishment at him. They had become spectators.

He turned to the front again. He saw, under the lifted smoke, a deserted ground.

He looked bewildered for a moment. Then there appeared upon the glazed emptiness of his eyes a diamond point of intelligence. "Oh," he said, understanding.

He returned to his comrades and threw himself upon the ground. He sprawled like a man who had been thrashed. His flesh seemed strangely on fire. The sounds of the battle continued in his ears. He groped blindly for his canteen.

The lieutenant was crowing. He seemed drunk with fighting. He called out to the youth, "By heavens, I wish I had ten thousand wild cats like you! I could tear the stomach out of this war in less than a week!" He puffed out his chest with large dignity as he said it.

Some of the men muttered and looked at the youth in awestruck ways. It was plain that they had found time to watch him. He had gone on loading and firing and cursing without stopping at all. And the men now looked upon him as a war devil.

The friend came staggering to him. There was some fright and dismay in his voice. "Are you all right, Fleming? Do you feel all right? There ain't nothin' the matter with you, Henry, is there?"

"No," said the youth with difficulty. His throat seemed full of knobs and burrs.

These incidents made the youth think. It was revealed to him that he had been a savage, a beast. He had fought like a pagan[1] who defends his beliefs.

Looking back, he saw that it was fine, wild, and, in some ways, easy. He had been a tremendous figure, no doubt. By this struggle, he had overcome obstacles which he had thought to be mountains. They had fallen like paper peaks.

He was now what he called a hero. And he had not been aware of the process. He had slept and, awakening, found himself a knight.

He lay and basked in the occasional stares of his comrades. Their faces were varied in degrees of blackness from the burned powder. Some were utterly smudged. They stank with perspiration, and their breaths came hard and wheezing. And from these soiled expanses they peered at him.

"Hot work! Hot work!" cried the lieutenant with excitement. He walked up and down, restless and eager. Sometimes his voice could be heard in a wild, **incomprehensible** laugh.

From time to time, he had a particularly wise thought upon the science of war. Without thinking, he always addressed himself to the youth.

There was some grim rejoicing by the men. "By thunder, I bet this army will never see another new regiment like us!"

"You bet!"

> "A dog, a woman, and a walnut tree,
> The more you beat 'em, the better they be!

That's like us."

"Lost a pile of men, they did. If an ol' woman swept

[1] A pagan is one who has little or no religion.

up the woods, she'd get a dustpanful.''

"Yes, and if she'll come around again in about an hour, she'll get a pile more.''

The forest still bore its burden of noise. From off under the trees came the rolling clatter of the musketry. Each distant thicket seemed a strange porcupine with quills of flame.

A cloud of dark smoke went up, as if from smoldering ruins. The sun was now bright and gay in the shiny blue sky.

Chapter 18

Vocabulary Preview

Below is a list of words that appear in this chapter. Review the list and get to know the words before you read the chapter.

abandon spirit; liveliness
dexterous skillful
edifice building
ladened burdened; weighed down
presume suppose; believe
reposeful restful; peaceful

The ragged line had relief for some minutes. But during its pause, the struggle in the forest became greater. At last, the trees seemed to quiver from the firing. The ground shook from the rushing of men.

The voices of the cannon were mingled in a low and endless row. It seemed difficult to live in such an atmosphere. The chests of the men strained for a bit of freshness. Their throats craved water.

There was one man shot through the body. He raised a cry of bitter pain when this lull came. Perhaps he had been calling out during the fighting also. At that time, no one had heard him. But now the men turned at the dreadful complaints of him upon the ground.

"Who is it? Who is it?"

"It's Jimmie Rogers. Jimmie Rogers."

When their eyes first saw him, there was a sudden halt. It was as if they feared to go near. He was thrashing about in the grass. He twisted his shuddering body into many strange postures. He was screaming loudly.

This instant's pause seemed to fill him with a tremendous, fantastic contempt. He damned them in shrieked sentences.

The youth's friend thought he remembered a stream being nearby. He obtained permission to go for some water. Immediately, canteens were showered upon him.

"Fill mine, will you?"

"Bring me some, too."

"And me, too."

He departed, **ladened.** The youth went with his friend. He felt a desire to throw his heated body onto the stream. Soaking there, he could drink quarts.

They made a hurried search for the supposed stream, but did not find it. "No water here," said the youth. They turned without delay and began to retrace their steps.

From their position, they again faced toward the place of the fighting. Before, their visions had been blurred by the hurling smoke of the line. Now they could, of course, view a greater amount of the battle.

They could see dark stretches winding along the land. On one cleared space, there was a row of guns making gray clouds. Large flashes of orange-colored flame filled the clouds.

Over some leaves, they could see the roof of a house. One window, glowing a deep murder red, shone squarely through the leaves. From the **edifice,** a tall, leaning tower of smoke went far into the sky.

Looking over their own troops, they saw mixed masses slowly getting into regular form. The sunlight made twinkling points of the bright steel. To the rear there was a glimpse of a distant roadway as it curved over a slope. It was crowded with retreating infantry.

From all the tangled forest arose the smoke and bluster of the battle. The air was always filled with a blaring.

Near where they stood, shells were flip-flapping and hooting. Occasional bullets buzzed in the air and smacked into tree trunks. Wounded men and other stragglers were slinking through the woods.

The youth and his companion looked down an aisle of the grove. They saw a jangling general and his staff almost ride upon a wounded man. He was crawling on his hands and knees.

The general reined strongly at his charger's opened and foamy mouth. He guided it with **dexterous** horsemanship past the man. The latter scrambled in wild and torturing haste.

His strength evidently failed him as he reached a place of safety. One of his arms suddenly weakened. He fell, sliding over upon his back. He lay stretched out, breathing gently.

A moment later, the small, creaking procession was directly in front of the two soldiers. Another officer rode with the skillful **abandon** of a cowboy. He galloped his horse to a position directly before the general.

The two unnoticed foot soldiers made a little show of going on. But they lingered near in the desire to overhear the conversation. Perhaps, they thought, some great inner historical thing would be said.

The boys knew the general as the commander of their division. He looked at the other officer and spoke coolly. It was as if he were criticizing his clothes.

"The enemy's formin' over there for another charge," he said. "It will be directed against Whiterside. I fear they'll break through there unless we work like thunder to stop them."

The other swore at his nervous horse, and then cleared his throat. He made a gesture toward his cap. "It will be hell to pay stoppin' them," he said shortly.

"I **presume** so," remarked the general. Then he began to talk quickly and in a lower tone. He often illustrated his words with a pointing finger. The two infantrymen could hear nothing until finally the general asked, "What troops can you spare?"

The officer who rode like a cowboy thought for an instant. "Well," he said, "I had to order in the 12th to help the 76th. I haven't really got any. But there's the 304th. They fight like a lot of mule drivers. I can spare them best of any."

The youth and his friend exchanged glances of astonishment.

The general spoke sharply. "Get 'em ready, then. I'll watch developments from here. I'll send you word when to start 'em. It will happen in five minutes."

The other officer tossed his fingers toward his cap and wheeled his horse, starting away. The general called out to him in a sober voice, "I don't believe many of your mule drivers will get back."

The other shouted something in reply. He smiled.

With scared faces, the youth and his companion hurried back to the line.

These happenings had occupied a very short time. Still, the youth felt that in them he had aged. New eyes were given to him. And the most startling thing was to learn suddenly that he was of minor importance.

The officer spoke of the regiment as if he referred to a broom. Some part of the woods needed sweeping, perhaps. He merely indicated a broom in a tone properly uncaring to its fate. It was war, no doubt, but it appeared strange.

The two boys approached the line. The lieutenant saw them and swelled with wrath. "Fleming—Wilson—how long does it take you to get water, anyhow? Where you been?"

But his lecture ceased as he saw their eyes, which were large with great tales. "We're goin' to charge—we're goin' to charge!" cried the youth's friend, hastening with his news.

"Charge?" said the lieutenant. "Charge? Well, by God! Now, this is real fightin'." Over his soiled face there went a boastful smile. "Charge? Well, by God!"

A little group of soldiers surrounded the two youths. "Are we, sure enough? Well, I'll be derned! Charge? What for? What at? Wilson, you're lyin'."

"I hope to die," said the youth's friend, speaking in a tone of angry protest. "Sure as shootin', I tell you."

And the youth spoke in re-enforcement. "Not by a blame sight, he ain't lyin'. We heard 'em talkin'."

They caught sight of two mounted figures a short distance from them. One was the colonel of the regiment. The other was the officer who had received orders from the commander of the division. They were gesturing at each other. The soldier, pointing at them, interpreted the scene.

One man had a final objection. "How could you hear 'em talkin'?"

But the men, for a large part, nodded. They admitted that the two friends had been speaking the truth before.

They settled back into **reposeful** attitudes. They had airs of having accepted the matter. And they thought upon it, with a hundred varieties of expression. It was a fascinating thing to think about. Many tightened their belts carefully and hitched at their trousers.

A moment later, the officers began to bustle among the men. They pushed them into a more compact mass and into a better position. They chased those that straggled. They fumed at a few men who seemed to show by their attitudes that they had decided to remain at that spot. The officers were like critical shepherds struggling with sheep.

Soon, the regiment seemed to draw itself up and heave a deep breath. None of the men's faces were mirrors of large thoughts. The soldiers were bended and stooped like sprinters before a signal.

Many pairs of glinting eyes peered from the grimy faces. They looked toward the curtains of the deeper woods. They seemed to be caught up in deep thoughts of time and distance.

They were surrounded by the noises of the monstrous quarrel between the two armies. The world was fully interested in other matters. Apparently, the regiment had its small affair to itself.

The youth, turning, shot a quick, inquiring glance at his friend. His friend returned to him the same manner of look. They were the only ones who possessed an inner knowledge. "Mule drivers—hell to pay—don't believe many will get back."

It was an ironical secret. Still, they saw no hesitation in each other's faces. They nodded a mute and unprotesting agreement when a shaggy man near them said in a meek voice, "We'll get swallowed."

Chapter 19

The youth stared at the land in front of him. Its growth now seemed to hide powers and horrors. He was unaware of the machinery of orders that started the charge. But from the corners of his eyes, he saw an officer who looked like a boy on horseback. He came galloping, waving his hat.

Suddenly, he felt a straining and heaving among the men. The line fell slowly forward like a toppling wall. With a **convulsive** gasp that was intended for a cheer, the regiment began its journey.

The youth was pushed and jostled for a moment before he understood the movement at all. But directly, he lunged ahead and began to run.

He fixed his eye upon a distant and noticeable clump of trees. He had figured the enemy was to be met there. He ran toward it as toward a goal. He had believed throughout that it was a mere question of getting over an unpleasant matter as quickly as possible. So he ran desperately, as if pursued for a murder.

His face was drawn hard and tight with the stress of his work. He fixed his eyes in an awful glare. His uniform was soiled and disordered. His red and inflamed features were topped off by the dingy rag with its spot of blood. His rifle swung and his other equipment banged. He looked to be an insane soldier.

The regiment swung from its position out into a cleared space. Soon the woods and thickets awakened. Yellow flames leaped toward the regiment from many directions. The forest made a tremendous objection.

The line lurched straight for a moment. Then the right wing swung forward. It, in turn, was surpassed by the left. Afterward, the center rushed to the front until the regiment was a wedge-shaped mass. But an instant later, the opposition of the bushes, trees, and uneven places on the ground split the command. They scattered it into detached clusters.

The youth, light-footed, was unknowingly in front. His eyes still kept note of the clump of trees. From all places near it, the united yell of the enemy could be heard. The little flames of rifles leaped from it.

The song of the bullets was in the air and shells snarled among the tree tops. One tumbled directly into the middle of a hurrying group. It exploded in a bright red fury. A man was almost over it. There was an instant's spectacle of him throwing up his hands to shield his eyes.

Other men were punched by bullets. They fell in **grotesque** agonies. The regiment left a connecting trail of bodies.

They had passed into a clearer atmosphere. There was an effect like a vision in the new appearance of the landscape. They could plainly see some men working madly at a battery.[1] The opposing infantry's lines were defined by the gray walls and fringes of smoke.

It seemed to the youth that he saw everything. Each blade of the green grass was bold and clear. He thought that he was aware of every change in the thin, **transparent** vapor that floated idly in sheets. The brown or gray trunks of the trees showed each roughness of their surfaces.

[1] Here the men are preparing their cannons to be ready for an attack.

The men of the regiment were running madly or falling. It was as if they were thrown headlong, to queer, heaped-up corpses. They had starting eyes and sweating faces. The youth could see each of them.

His mind took a mechanical but firm impression. So afterward, everything was pictured and explained to him, save why he himself was there.

But there was a frenzy made from this furious rush. The men were pitching forward insanely. Now they had burst into cheerings, moblike and savage. They were tuned in strange keys that can awaken the idiot and the **stoic.** It made a mad enthusiasm which seemed unstoppable even before granite and brass.

There was the madness that encounters despair and death. It is careless and blind to the odds. It is a temporary but noble absence of selfishness. Perhaps this unselfishness explained something. It might have been the reason the youth wondered, afterward, what reasons he could have had for being there.

Soon the straining pace ate up the energies of the men. As if by agreement, the leaders began to slacken their speed. The volleys directed against them had had a seeming windlike effect.

The regiment snorted and blew. Among some **stolid** trees, it began to falter and hesitate. The men stared intently. They began to wait for some of the distant walls of smoke to move and show them the scene. Much of their strength and their breath had vanished. Now they returned to caution. They were become men again.

The youth had a vague belief that he had run miles. He thought, in a way, that he was now in some new and unknown land.

The regiment ceased its advance. At that moment, the protesting splutter of musketry became a steadied roar. Long and accurate fringes of smoke spread out. From the top of a small hill came level belchings of yellow flame. They caused an inhuman whistling in the air.

The men halted. They had an opportunity to see some of their comrades dropping with moans and shrieks. A few lay under foot, still or wailing. And now for an instant, the men stood and watched the regiment dwindle. Their rifles were slack in their hands.

The men appeared dazed and stupid. This spectacle seemed to paralyze them. It overcame them with a fatal charm. They stared woodenly at the sights. Then, lowering their eyes, they looked from face to face. It was a strange pause, and a strange silence.

Then arose the roar of the lieutenant. His voice came above the sounds of the outside commotion. He strode suddenly forth, his childish features black with rage.

"Come on, you fools!" he bellowed. "Come on! You can't stay here. You must come on." He said more, but much of it could not be understood.

He started rapidly forward, with his head turned toward the men. "Come on," he was shouting. The men stared with blank and yokel-like eyes at him. The lieutenant was forced to halt and retrace his steps.

He stood, then, with his back to the enemy. He delivered enormous curses into the faces of the men. His body vibrated from the weight and force of his swearing. And he could string oaths with the ease of a maiden who strings beads.

The friend of the youth was aroused. He lurched suddenly forward and dropped to his knees. He fired an angry shot at the stubborn woods. This action awakened the men. They huddled no more like sheep. They seemed suddenly to remember their weapons. They at once began firing.

Hounded by their officers, they began to move forward. The regiment was like a cart caught in mud and muddle. It started unevenly with many jolts and jerks. The men stopped now every few paces to fire and load. In this manner, they moved slowly on from trees to trees.

The flaming opposition in front of them grew with their advance. At last, it seemed that all forward ways were barred by the thin leaping tongues. Off to the right, a threatening skirmish could sometimes be dimly seen.

The smoke that had lately developed was in confusing clouds. It made it difficult for the regiment to proceed with intelligence. As he passed through each curling mass, the youth wondered what would confront him on the farther side.

The command went painfully forward. An open space came between them and the fiery lines. The men crouched and cringed behind some trees. They clung there with desperation, as if threatened by a wave. They looked wild-eyed. It was as if they were amazed at this furious disturbance they had stirred.

In the storm, there was a mocking expression of their importance. The faces of the men, too, showed a lack of a certain feeling of responsibility for being there. It was as if they had been driven. Like animals, they failed to remember the cause of their situation. The whole affair seemed impossible to understand for many of them.

As they halted thus, the lieutenant again began to bellow savagely. He paid no attention to the vicious threats of the bullets. He just went about coaxing, scolding, and bedamning.

His lips were usually in a soft and childlike curve. But now they twisted into unholy shapes. He swore by all possible gods.

Once he grabbed the youth by the arm. "Come on, you lunkhead!" he roared. "Come on! We'll all get killed if we stay here. We've only got to go across that lot. And then—" But the remainder of his idea disappeared in a blue haze of curses.

The youth stretched forth his arm. "Cross there?" His mouth was puckered in doubt and awe.

"Certainly. Just cross the lot! We can't stay here," screamed the lieutenant. He poked his face close to the youth and waved his bandaged hand. "Come on!"

Soon, he grappled with him as if for a wrestling bout. It was as if he planned to drag the youth by the ear on to the assault.

The private felt a sudden unspeakable **indignation** against his officer. He twisted fiercely and shook him off.

"Come on yourself, then," he yelled. There was a bitter challenge in his voice.

They galloped together down the regimental front. The

friend scrambled after them. In front of the colors, the three men began to bawl, ''Come on! Come on!''

They danced and spun like tortured savages.

The flag was obedient to these appeals. It bent its glittering form and swept toward them. The men wavered in indecision for a moment. Then, with a long, wailful cry, the battered regiment surged forward. It began its new journey.

Over the field went the scurrying mass. It was a handful of men splattered into the faces of the enemy. Toward it instantly sprang the yellow tongues. A vast quantity of blue smoke hung before them. A mighty banging made ears valueless.

The youth ran like a madman to reach the woods before a bullet could discover him. He ducked his head low, like a football player. In his haste, his eyes almost closed. The scene was a wild blur. Quivering saliva stood at the corners of his mouth.

He hurled himself forward. And within him was born a love, a despairing fondness for this flag which was near him. It was a creation of beauty and deathlessness. It was a radiant goddess that bended its form with a proud gesture to him.

The flag was a woman, red and white, hating and loving. It called him with the voice of his hopes. Because no harm could come to it, he gave it power. He kept near, as if it could be a saver of lives. A pleading cry went from his mind.

In the mad scramble, he was aware that the color sergeant[2] flinched suddenly. It was as if he had been struck by a club. He faltered, and then became motionless, save for his quivering knees.

The youth made a spring and a clutch at the pole. At the same instant, his friend grabbed it from the other side. They jerked at it, bold and furious. But the color sergeant was dead. The corpse would not give up its trust.

For a moment there was a grim meeting. The dead man swung with bended back. He seemed to be stubbornly tug-

[2]The color sergeant carries the flag.

ging, in ridiculous and awful ways, for the possession of the flag.

It was past in an instant of time. They jerked the flag furiously from the dead man. As they turned again, the corpse swayed forward with bowed head. One arm swung high. The curved hand fell with heavy protest on the friend's unheeding shoulder.

Chapter 20

Vocabulary Preview

Below is a list of words that appear in this chapter.
Review the list and get to know the words before
you read the chapter.

emblem flag; banner
perilous dangerous
remorse sorrow; regret
rift split; opening
treachery betrayal; falseness
turmoil confusion; disorder

When the two youths turned with the flag, they saw that
much of the regiment had crumbled away. The sad portion
that was left was coming slowly back.

The men had hurled themselves like missiles. Now they
had spent their forces. They slowly retreated, with their faces
still toward the spluttering woods. Their hot rifles still replied
to the noise. Several officers were giving orders, their voices
rising to screams.

"Where in hell you goin'?" the lieutenant was asking in
a sarcastic howl.

And a red-bearded officer's brassy voice could plainly
be heard. He was commanding, "Shoot into 'em! Shoot into
'em! God damn their souls!"

There was a jumble of screeches. The men were ordered
to do conflicting and impossible things.

The youth and his friend had a small scuffle over the flag.

"Give it to me!"

"No, let me keep it!"

Each felt satisfied that the other held it. But each felt bound to declare his willingness to further risk himself. And each did so by offering to carry the **emblem.** The youth roughly pushed his friend away.

The regiment fell back to the stolid trees. There it halted for a moment. It fired at some dark forms that had begun to steal upon its track.

Soon it resumed its march again, curving among the tree trunks. The shrinking regiment again reached the first open space. By then, they were receiving a fast fire that showed no mercy. There seemed to be mobs all about them.

The greater part of the men were discouraged. Their spirits were worn by the **turmoil.** They acted as if stunned. They accepted the pelting of the bullets with bowed and weary heads.

It was of no purpose to strive against walls. It was of no use to batter themselves against granite. Now they knew that they had tried to conquer an unconquerable thing. This gave them a feeling that they had been betrayed.

They frowned with bent brows, but dangerously, upon some of the officers. They frowned particularly upon the red-bearded one with the brassy voice.

However, the rear of the regiment had a few men left. They continued to shoot madly at the advancing foes. They seemed determined to make every trouble.

The youthful lieutenant was perhaps the last man in the disordered mass. His forgotten back was toward the enemy. He had been shot in the arm. It hung straight and rigid.

Occasionally, he would forget about it. He would try to emphasize an oath with a sweeping gesture. The increased pain caused him to swear with incredible power.

The youth went along with slipping, unsure feet. He kept watchful eyes toward the rear. A scowl of shame and rage was upon his face. He had thought of a fine revenge upon the officer who had referred to him and his fellows as mule drivers.

But he saw that it could not come to pass. His dreams had collapsed. The mule drivers had dwindled quickly. They had wavered and hesitated on the little clearing and then had pulled back. And now the retreat of the mule drivers was a march of shame to him.

A dagger-pointed gaze from without the youth's blackened face was held toward the enemy. But his greater hatred was placed elsewhere. It was directed against the man who, not knowing him, had called him a mule driver.

He knew that he and his comrades had failed. They had done nothing successfully that might bring the little pangs of **remorse** upon the officer. The youth allowed the rage of the confused to possess him.

That cold officer saw himself as high and mighty. He dropped his labels on people without showing any concern. He would be finer as a dead man, the youth thought. He felt it was terrible that he would never get the secret right to torment him back.

The youth had pictured red letters of curious revenge. "We *are* mule drivers, are we?" But now he had to throw them away.

He soon wrapped his heart in the cloak of his pride. He kept the flag upright. He shouted at his fellows, pushing against their chests with his free hand. To those he knew well, he made frantic appeals. He called them by name.

The lieutenant was scolding and near to losing his mind with rage. Between him and the youth, there was felt a subtle fellowship and equality. They supported each other in all manner of hoarse, howling protests.

But the regiment was a machine run down. The two men babbled at a forceless thing. Some soldiers had heart to go slowly. But they were continually shaken in their determination. They knew that comrades were slipping with speed back to the lines.

It was difficult to think of reputations when others were thinking of skins. Wounded men were left crying on this black journey.

The smoke borders and flames blustered always. The youth peered once through a sudden **rift** in a cloud. He saw a brown mass of troops. They were blended and enlarged until they appeared to be thousands. A fierce-colored flag flashed before his vision.

Then it was as if the uplifting of the smoke had been prearranged. Immediately, the discovered troops burst into a rasping yell. A hundred flames jetted toward the retreating band.

A rolling gray cloud again arose as the regiment doggedly replied. The youth had to depend again upon his misused ears. They were trembling and buzzing from the racket of musketry and yells.

The way seemed eternal. In the clouded haze, men became stricken with panic. They thought that the regiment had lost its path and was going in a **perilous** direction.

The men who headed the wild march turned. They came pushing back against their comrades, screaming that they were being fired upon. They believed the shots came from points which they thought were their own lines.

At this cry, a mad fear and dismay overcame the troops. One soldier had, until now, wanted to make the regiment into a wise little band. He thought they would proceed calmly amid the huge-appearing difficulties. But now he suddenly sank down and buried his face in his arms. He had an air of bowing to a doom.

From another soldier, a shrill cry of grief rang out. It was filled with profane comments about a general. Men ran here and there. They sought with their eyes roads of escape. With calm regularity, bullets buffed into men. It was as if they were controlled by a schedule.

The youth walked stolidly into the midst of the mob. With his flag in his hands, he took a stand. It was as if he expected an attempt to push him to the ground. He unconsciously took on the attitude of the color bearer in the fight of the day before.

He passed over his brow a hand that trembled. His breath did not come freely. He was choking during this small wait for the crisis.

His friend came to him. "Well, Henry, I guess this is good-bye—John."

"Oh, shut up, you damned fool!" replied the youth. He would not look at the other.

The officers labored like public servants. They tried to

beat the mass into a proper circle to face the enemy. The ground was uneven and torn. The men curled into low places. They fitted themselves snugly behind whatever would stop a bullet.

The lieutenant was standing quietly. He had his legs far apart and his sword held in the manner of a cane. The youth noted him with vague surprise. He wondered what had happened to his vocal organs that he no more cursed.

There was something strange in this little intent pause of the lieutenant. He was like a babe who, having wept its fill, raises its eyes and fixes upon a distant toy. The lieutenant was caught up in his thoughts. His soft under lip quivered from self-whispered words.

Some lazy and ignorant smoke curled slowly. The men hid from the bullets. They waited eagerly for the smoke to lift and reveal the situation of the regiment.

The silent ranks were suddenly thrilled by the eager voice of the youthful lieutenant. He bawled out, "Here they come! Right onto us, by God!" His further words were lost in a roar of wicked thunder from the men's rifles.

The youth's eyes had instantly turned in the direction indicated by the awakened and agitated lieutenant. He had seen the haze of **treachery** revealing a body of enemy soldiers. They were so near that he could see their features.

There was a recognition as he looked at the types of faces. Also, he could see with dim amazement that their uniforms were rather gay in effect. They were light gray, accented with a brilliant-colored facing. In addition, the clothes seemed new.

These troops had appeared to be going forward with caution. They held their rifles ready. Then the youthful lieutenant saw them. Their movement was slowed by the firing from the blue regiment.

They could only be glimpsed for a moment. But it could be seen that they had not been aware of how close they were to their dark-suited foes. Or else they had mistaken the direction.

Almost instantly, they were shut utterly from the youth's sight by the smoke from the energetic rifles of his companions. He strained his vision to learn what the shooting had accomplished. But the smoke hung before him.

The two bodies of troops exchanged blows. They acted in the manner of a pair of boxers. The fast angry firing went back and forth. The men in blue were intent with the despair of their circumstances. They seized upon the revenge to be had at close range.

Their thunder swelled loud and valiant. Their curving front bristled with flashes. The place echoed with the ringing of their ramrods.

The youth ducked and dodged for a time. He achieved a few poor views of the enemy. There appeared to be many of them and they were replying swiftly.

They seemed to be moving toward the blue regiment, step by step. The youth seated himself sadly on the ground with his flag between his knees.

He noted the vicious, wolflike temper of his comrades. At the same time, he had a sweet thought. The enemy was about to swallow the regimental broom as a large prisoner. But the broom could at least have the pleasure of going down with bristles forward.

But the blows of the enemy began to grow more weak. Fewer bullets ripped the air. Finally, the men slowed down to learn of the fight. They could see only dark, floating smoke.

The regiment lay still and gazed. Soon, some chance whim came to the pestering blur. It began to coil heavily away.

The men saw a ground vacant of fighters. It would have been an empty stage. But there were a few corpses that lay thrown and twisted into fantastic shapes upon the ground.

At the sight of this scene, many of the men in blue sprang from behind their covers. They made an awkward dance of joy. Their eyes burned and a hoarse cheer of triumph broke from their dry lips.

It had begun to seem to them that events were trying to prove that they were helpless. These little battles had evidently tried to demonstrate that the men could not fight well.

They had been on the verge of giving in to these opinions. But this small duel had shown them that the odds were not impossible. And by it, they had revenged themselves upon their self-doubts and upon the foe.

The energy of enthusiasm was theirs again. They gazed about them with looks of uplifted pride. They felt new trust in the grim, always confident weapons in their hands. And they were men.

Chapter 21

Vocabulary Preview

Below is a list of words that appear in this chapter. Review the list and get to know the words before you read the chapter.

depleted worn out; exhausted
diversion distraction; act of drawing attention away from something
exertions efforts; struggles
insignificant of little importance
tranquil quiet; untroubled
vexation anger

Soon, they knew that no firing threatened them. All ways seemed once more opened to them. The dusty blue lines of their friends were revealed a short distance away.

In the distance there were many very loud noises. But in all this part of the field there was a sudden stillness. They could see that they were free. The **depleted** band drew a long breath of relief. It gathered itself into a bunch to complete its trip.

In this last length of journey, the men began to show strange emotions. They hurried with nervous fear. Some had been dark and unfaltering in the grimmest moments. But now they could not conceal an anxiety that made them frantic.

It was, perhaps, that the times for proper military deaths had passed. Now they dreaded to be killed in **insignificant** ways. Or, perhaps, they thought it would be too ironical to get killed at the edge of safety. With backward looks of uneasiness, they hastened.

The soldiers approached their own lines. There was some sarcasm shown by a thin and bronzed regiment that lay resting in the shade of trees. Questions floated toward them.

"Where the hell you been?"

"What you comin' back for?"

"Why didn't you stay there?"

"Was it warm out there, sonny?"

"Goin' home now, boys?"

One shouted in cutting imitation, "Oh, mother, come quick and look at the soldiers!"

There was no reply from the bruised and battered regiment. One man, however, made broadcast challenges to fist fights. The red-bearded officer walked rather near. He glared in great swashbuckler[1] style at a tall captain in the other regiment.

The lieutenant stopped the man who wished to fist fight. And the tall captain flushed at the little display of the red-bearded one. He was obliged to look intently at some trees.

The youth's tender flesh was deeply stung by these remarks. From under his creased brows he glowered with hate at the mockers. He thought about a few revenges.

Still, many in the regiment hung their heads in criminal fashion. It came to pass that the men trudged with sudden heaviness. It was as if they bore upon their bended shoulders the coffin of their honor. And the youthful lieutenant remembered himself. He began to mutter softly in black curses.

They turned when they arrived at their old position. They looked toward the ground over which they had charged.

The youth thought this over and was struck with a large astonishment. He discovered that the distances were small and foolish. They could not compare with the brilliant measurings of his mind.

The stolid trees, where much had taken place, seemed incredibly near. The time, too, now that he reflected, he saw

[1]A swashbuckler is a bold, boastful character.

to have been short.

He wondered at the number of emotions and events. How had they been crowded into such little spaces? Elflike thoughts must have exaggerated and enlarged everything, he said.

It seemed, then, that there was bitter justice in the speeches of the thin and bronzed veterans. He hid a glance of disdain at his fellows who strewed the ground. They were choking with dust, red from perspiration, misty-eyed, and rumpled.

They were gulping at their canteens, fiercely trying to wring every bit of water from them. They polished at their swollen and watery features with coat sleeves and bunches of grass.

However, the youth thought back upon his performance during the charge. He found great joy in this. He had had very little time before in which to appreciate himself. There was now much satisfaction in quietly thinking of his actions. He recalled bits of colors. In the flurry, they had stamped themselves unawares upon his engaged senses.

The regiment lay heaving from its hot **exertions.** The officer who had named them as mule drivers came galloping along the line. He had lost his cap. His windblown hair streamed wildly. His face was dark with **vexation** and wrath.

His temper was displayed with more clearness by the way in which he managed his horse. He jerked and twisted savagely at his bridle. He stopped the hard-breathing animal with a furious pull near the colonel of the regiment.

He immediately exploded into criticisms. These came to the ears of the men uninvited. They were suddenly alert. They were always curious about black words between officers.

"Oh, thunder, MacChesnay! What an awful bull you made of this thing!" began the officer. He attempted low tones. But his anger caused certain of the men to learn the sense of his words.

"What an awful mess you made! Good Lord, man, you stopped about a hundred feet this side of a very pretty success! Your men should have gone a hundred feet farther.

You would have made a great charge. But as it is—what a lot of mud diggers you've got anyway!"

The men listened with their breaths held. They now turned their curious eyes upon the colonel. They had a childlike interest in this affair.

The colonel was seen to straighten his form. He put one hand forth in an impressive fashion. He wore an injured air. It was as if a preacher had been accused of stealing. The men were wiggling in a rejoicing of excitement.

But all of a sudden, the colonel's manner changed from that of a preacher to that of a Frenchman. He shrugged his shoulders. "Oh, well, general, we went as far as we could," he said calmly.

"As far as you could? Did you, by God?" snorted the other. "Well, that wasn't very far, was it?" he added, with a glance of cold contempt into the other's eyes.

"Not very far, I think," he continued. "You were supposed to make a **diversion** in favor of Whiterside. How well you succeeded your own ears can now tell you." He wheeled his horse and rode stiffly away.

The colonel was now forced to hear the jarring noises of a battle in the woods to the left. He broke out in vague damnations.

The lieutenant had listened with an air of helpless rage to the interview. He spoke suddenly in firm and confident tones. "I don't care what a man is—whether he is a general or what. If he says the boys didn't put up a good fight out there, he's a damned fool."

"Lieutenant," began the colonel, severely, "this is my own affair. And I'll trouble you—"

The lieutenant made an obedient gesture. "All right, colonel, all right," he said. He sat down with an air of being content with himself.

The news that the regiment had been reproached went along the line. For a time the men were puzzled by it. "Good thunder!" they exclaimed, staring at the vanishing form of the general. They thought it to be a huge mistake.

Soon, however, they began to believe that in truth their efforts had been called light. The youth could see this feeling weigh upon the entire regiment. At last, the men were like cuffed and cursed animals, but uncontrollable for all that.

The friend, with an outrage in his eye, went to the youth. "I wonder what he does want," he said. "He must think we went out there and played marbles! I never saw such a man!"

The youth developed a **tranquil** philosophy for these moments of hard feelings. "Oh, well," he answered. "He probably didn't see nothing of it at all and got mad as blazes. And he concluded we were a lot of sheep, just because we didn't do what he wanted done.

"It's a pity old Grandpa Henderson got killed yesterday. He'd have known that we did our best and fought good. It's just our awful luck, that's what."

"I should say so," replied the friend. He seemed to be deeply wounded at an injustice. "I should say we did have awful luck! There's no fun in fightin' for people when everything you do—no matter what—ain't done right. I have a notion to stay behind next time. They can take their ol' charge and go to the devil with it."

The youth spoke soothingly to his comrade. "Well, we both did good. I'd like to see the fool what'd say we both didn't do as good as we could."

"Of course we did," declared the friend boldly. "And I'd break the feller's neck if he was as big as a church. But we're all right, anyhow. For I heard one feller say that we two fought the best in the regiment. And they had a great argument about it.

"Another feller, of course," continued the friend, "he had to up and say it was a lie. He seen all what was goin' on and he never seen us from the beginnin' to the end. And a lot more struck in and says it wasn't a lie. We did fight like thunder. And they give us quite a send-off.

"But this is what I can't stand—these everlastin' ol' soldiers, titterin' and laughin'. And then that general, he's crazy."

The youth exclaimed with sudden anger, "He's a lunkhead! He makes me mad. I wish he'd come along next time. We'd show him what—"

He quit because several men had come hurrying up. Their faces expressed a bringing of great news.

"O Flem, you just oughta heard!" cried one, eagerly.

"Heard what?" said the youth.

"You just oughta heard!" repeated the other. And he arranged himself to tell his story. The others made an excited circle.

"Well, sir, the colonel met your lieutenant right by us. It was the damnedest thing I ever heard. And he says, 'Ahem! Ahem!' he says. 'Mr. Hasbrouck!' he says, 'by the way, who was that lad what carried the flag?' he says.

"There, Flemin', what do you think of that? 'Who was the lad what carried the flag?' he says. And the lieutenant, he speaks up right away, 'That's Flemin', and he's a jimhickey,' he says, right away.

"What? I say he did. 'A jimhickey,' he says. Those are his words. He did, too. I say he did. If you can tell this story better than I can, go ahead and tell it. Well, then, keep your mouth shut.[2]

"The lieutenant, he says, 'He's a jimhickey.'

"And the colonel, he says: 'Ahem! Ahem! He is, indeed, a very good man to have, ahem! He kept the flag way to the front. I saw him. He's a good one,' says the colonel.

" 'You bet,' says the lieutenant, 'he and a feller named Wilson was at the head of the charge. They was howlin' like Indians all the time,' he says. 'Head of the charge all the time,' he says. 'A feller named Wilson,' he says.

"There, Wilson, my boy. Put that in a letter and send it home to your mother, hay?

" 'A feller named Wilson,' he says.

"And the colonel, he says, 'Were they, indeed? Ahem! Ahem! My sakes!' he says. 'At the head of the regiment?' he says.

" 'They were,' says the lieutenant.

" 'My sakes!' says the colonel. He says, 'Well, well, well,' he says. 'Those two babies?'

[2]As Thompson is talking, his companions are criticizing the way he describes these events.

" 'They were,' says the lieutenant.

" 'Well, well,' says the colonel. 'They deserve to be major generals.' " [3]

The youth and his friend had said, "Huh!"

"You're lyin', Thompson."

"Oh, go to blazes!"

"He never said it."

"Oh, what a lie!"

"Huh!"

They scoffed with youthful embarrassment. But despite this, they knew that their faces were deeply flushing from thrills of pleasure. They exchanged a secret glance of joy and congratulation.

They soon forgot many things. The past held no pictures of error and disappointment. They were very happy. Their hearts swelled with grateful affection for the colonel and the youthful lieutenant.

[3] See the military chart on page 147.

Chapter 22 (Summary)

The enemy again began to pour from the woods. But now the youth felt calm and self-confident. He watched the attack begin. He was relieved to finally see where some of the noises came from.

The youth saw regiments and brigades fiercely fighting in every direction. Every now and then he glimpsed groups of artillerymen.

Gradually the battle slowed down, and then the woods were silent. The blue lines waited and watched uneasily. Suddenly a sputtering of gunfire started up in the woods and quickly became deafening.

The youth watched men rushing wildly backward and forward. The opposing armies cast blow after blow upon each other. First one side, then the other sent up a winning yell. The battle flags flew in many directions. The youth couldn't tell who was winning.

When its time came, the youth's regiment charged furiously. The men fought like demons. The youth was still the color bearer. He could do little but watch the fighting.

A line of the enemy came within close range. The youth's comrades aimed their rifles and fired at the foes. But the enemy slid safely behind a fence and began to fire back at the blue lines.

The men of the blue regiment were grimly determined to keep their ground. They fought savagely.

The youth decided to stand firm no matter what happened. He was sure he would die. But to him this would be the perfect vengeance against the officer who had called the youth's regiment "mule drivers" and "mud diggers."

The regiment bled and men began to drop. The youth looked for his friend Wilson and found him alive and covered with powder. The lieutenant was also unhurt, but his curses were becoming weaker. Indeed, the entire regiment was quickly losing its strength.

Chapter 23

Vocabulary Preview

Below is a list of words that appear in this chapter. Review the list and get to know the words before you read the chapter.

collision clash; impact
dejection gloominess; sadness
formidable strong; powerful
resolution purpose; determination
scathing bitter; harsh
vanities boastings; braggings

The colonel came running along back of the line. There were other officers following him.

"We must charge 'em!" they shouted. "We must charge 'em!" they cried with resentful voices. It was as if they expected a revolt against this plan by the men.

The youth heard the shouts. He began to study the distance between him and the enemy. He made vague calculations. He saw that, to be firm soldiers, they must go forward.

It would be death to stay in the present place. And with all the circumstances, to go backward would honor too many others. Their hope was to push the stubborn foes away from the fence.

The youth's companions were weary and stiffened. He expected they would have to be driven to this attack. But then he turned towards them. He saw with a certain surprise that they were giving quick and sincere expressions of agreement.

There was an ominous, clanging overture[1] to the charge. The shafts of the bayonets rattled upon the rifle barrels. At the yelled words of command, the soldiers sprang forward in eager leaps.

There was new and unexpected force in the movement of the regiment. A knowledge of its faded and exhausted condition made the charge appear like an outburst. It was a display of strength that comes before a final feebleness. The men scampered in an insane fever of haste. They raced as if to achieve a sudden success before an energizing fluid should leave them.

It was a blind and despairing rush by the collection of men in dusty and tattered blue. They went over a green field and under a deep blue sky toward a fence, dimly outlined in smoke. Behind it spluttered the fierce rifles of the enemies.

The youth kept the bright colors to the front. He was waving his free arm in furious circles. All the while, he shrieked mad calls and appeals. He urged on those that did not need to be urged.

The mob of blue men hurled themselves on the dangerous group of rifles. It seemed that they were again grown suddenly wild with an enthusiasm of unselfishness.

Many firings started toward them. It looked as if the men would merely succeed in making a great sprinkling of corpses. They would be scattered on the grass between their former position and the fence.

But the men were in a state of frenzy. Perhaps this was because of forgotten **vanities.** They made a show of sublime recklessness.

There was no obvious questioning, nor figurings, nor diagrams. There were, apparently, no considered loopholes. It appeared that the swift wings of their desires would have shattered against the iron gates of the impossible.

The youth himself felt the daring spirit of a religion-mad savage. He was capable of great sacrifices, a tremendous death. He had no time to really consider. But he knew what

[1]An overture is a piece of music that is played before a play, opera, or other theatrical event begins. Overtures introduce the audience to the mood of the staged presentation.

he thought. Bullets were only things that could prevent him from reaching the place of his attempt. There were subtle flashings of joy within him that he should be of this mind.

He strained all his strength. His eyesight was shaken and dazzled by the tension of thought and muscle. He did not see anything excepting the mist of smoke. This was gashed by the little knives of fire. But he knew that in it lay the aged fence of a vanished farmer. It protected the snuggled bodies of the gray men.

As he ran, a thought of the shock of contact gleamed in his mind. He expected a great **collision** when the two bodies of troops crashed together.

This became a part of his wild battle madness. He could feel the onward swing of the regiment about him. He imagined a thunderous, crushing blow. It would wipe out the enemy and spread worry and amazement for miles. The flying regiment was going to have the effect of a catapult.[2]

This dream made him run faster among his comrades. They were giving vent to hoarse and frantic cheers. But soon he could see that many of the men in gray did not intend to take the blow.

The smoke rolled. It revealed men who ran, their faces still turned. These grew to a crowd, who retired suddenly. Individuals wheeled often to send a bullet at the blue wave.

But at one part of the line, there was a grim and stubborn group. They made no movement. They were settled firmly down behind posts and rails. A flag, ruffled and fierce, waved over them. Their rifles sounded fiercely.

The blue whirl of men got very near. At last it seemed that, in truth, there would be a close and frightful scuffle. There was an expressed disdain in the opposition of the little group.

This scorn changed the meaning of the cheers of the men in blue. They became yells of wrath, directed personally. The cries of the two groups were now in sound an exchange of **scathing** insults.

Those in blue showed their teeth. Their eyes shone all

[2] A catapult is a device that flings or hurls large objects at a target.

white. They launched themselves at the throats of those who stood resisting. The space between dwindled to a minor distance.

The youth had centered the gaze of his soul upon that other flag. Its possession would be high pride. It would express blood minglings, near blows.

He had a great hatred for those who made extreme difficulties and complications. They caused the flag to be as a craved treasure of mythology.[3] It hung amid tasks and devices of danger.

He plunged like a mad horse at it. He was determined it should not escape if wild blows and darings of blows could seize it. His own emblem, quivering and aflare, was winging toward the other. It seemed there would shortly be a meeting of strange beaks and claws. It was as if they were eagles.

The swirling body of men came to a sudden halt at close and dangerous range. They roared a swift volley. The group in gray was split and broken by this fire. Even though they were filled with bullets, they still fought. The men in blue yelled again and rushed in upon it.

The youth leaped about. He saw, as through a mist, a picture of four or five men stretched upon the ground or writhing upon their knees with bowed heads. It was as if they had been stricken by bolts from the sky.

Tottering among them was the rival color bearer. The youth saw that he had been bitten vitally by the bullets of the last **formidable** volley. He knew this man was fighting a last struggle. It was the struggle of one whose legs are grasped by demons.

It was a horrible struggle. Over his face was the bleach of death. But set upon it were the dark and hard lines of desperate purpose. With this terrible grin of **resolution,** he hugged his precious flag to him. He stumbled and staggered. He tried to go the way that led to safety for it.

But his wounds always made it seem that his feet were

---

[3]A common theme in mythology is the search for treasure. This quest usually involves struggle and danger. An example of such an adventure is Jason's search for the golden fleece.

slow and held. He fought a grim fight, as with invisible fiends fastened greedily upon his limbs. Those in front of the scampering blue men howled cheers. They leaped at the fence. The despair of the lost was in his eyes as he glanced back at them.

The youth's friend went over the obstacle in a tumbling heap. He sprang at the flag as a panther at prey. He pulled at it and wrenched it free. He swung up its red brilliancy with a mad cry of victory.

At that moment the color bearer gasped. He lurched over in a final agony. He stiffened, twisted, and turned his dead face to the ground. There was much blood upon the grass blades.

At the place of success there began more wild uproars of cheers. The men waved their arms and bellowed in an ecstasy. When they spoke, it was as if they considered their listener to be a mile away. What hats and caps were left to them they often slung high in the air.

At one part of the line, four men had been swooped upon. They now sat as prisoners. Some blue men were about them in an eager and curious circle. The soldiers had trapped strange birds, and there was an examination. A flurry of fast questions was in the air.

One of the prisoners was nursing a slight wound in the foot. He cuddled it baby-wise. But he looked up from it often to curse with an amazing recklessness at the noses of his captors.

He told them to go to red regions. He called upon the disease-bringing wrath of strange gods. And with it all, he was alone. He was free from recognition of the finer points of the conduct of prisoners of war. It was as if a clumsy clod had trod upon his toe. And he thought it to be his privilege, his duty, to use deep, resentful oaths.

Another was a boy in years. He took his plight with great calmness and apparent good nature. He talked with the men in blue. He studied their faces with his bright and keen eyes.

They spoke of battles and conditions. There was a sharp interest in all their faces during this exchange of viewpoints. It seemed a great satisfaction to hear voices from where all had been darkness and imagination.

The third captive sat with an unhappy face. He maintained a stoical and cold attitude. To all advances he made one reply without change, "Ah, go to hell!"

The last of the four was always silent. For the most part, he kept his face turned in undisturbed directions. From the views the youth received, he seemed to be in a state of absolute **dejection.**

Shame was upon this last captive. With it was a deep regret that he was, perhaps, no more to be counted in the ranks of his fellows. The youth could detect no expression in him. Perhaps he was thinking about his narrowed future, the pictured dungeons, and starvations and brutalities.

These were likely to cross the imagination. But all the youth could see was shame for captivity and regret for the right to threaten.

The men had their fill of celebration. They settled down behind the old rail fence. They went to the opposite side to the one from which their foes had been driven. A few shot without accuracy at distant marks.

There was some long grass. The youth nestled in it and rested. He made a convenient rail support the flag. His friend was jubilant and glorified. Holding his treasure with vanity, he came to the youth there. They sat side by side and congratulated each other.

Chapter 24

The roarings had stretched in a long line of sound across the face of the forest. They began to grow **intermittent** and weaker. The loud voices of the artillery continued in some distant battle. But the crashes of the musketry had almost ceased.

The youth and his friend suddenly looked up. They felt a deadened form of distress as the noises, which had become a part of life, faded away.

They could see changes going on among the troops. There were marchings this way and that. A battery wheeled leisurely. On the top of a small hill was the thick gleam of many departing muskets.

The youth arose. "Well, what now, I wonder?" he said. By his tone, he seemed to be preparing to resent some new savagery in the way of noises and smashes. He shaded his eyes with his grimy hand and gazed over the field.

His friend also arose and stared. "I bet we're goin' to

get along out of this and back over the river," said he.

"Well, I'll swear!" said the youth.

They waited, watching. Within a little while, the regiment received orders to retrace its way. The men got up grunting from the grass, regretting the soft restfulness. They jerked their stiffened legs and stretched their arms over their heads. One man swore as he rubbed his eyes.

They all groaned "O Lord!" They had as many objections to this change as they would have had to a proposal for a new battle.

They trampled slowly back over the field across which they had run in a mad scamper.

The regiment marched until it had joined its fellows. The brigade reformed into a column and aimed through a wood at the road. Soon, they were in a mass of dust-covered troops. They were trudging along in a way parallel to the enemy's lines. These had been defined in the recent fighting.

They passed within view of a stolid white house. They saw in front of it groups of their comrades, lying in wait behind a neat wall of defense.

A row of guns was booming at a distant enemy. Shells thrown in reply were raising clouds of dust and splinters. Horsemen dashed along the line of defense.

At this point in its march, the division curved away from the field. It went winding off in the direction of the river. The significance of this movement impressed itself upon the youth.

He turned his head toward the trampled and rubbish-strewed ground. He breathed a breath of new satisfaction. He finally nudged his friend. "Well, it's all over," he said to him.

His friend gazed backward. "By God, it is," he agreed. They mused.

For a time the youth was forced to reflect in a puzzled and uncertain way. His mind was undergoing a subtle change. It took moments for it to cast off its battlefield ways. Then it resumed its accustomed course of thought.

Gradually, his brain emerged from the clogged clouds. At last he was able to more closely understand himself and

:ircumstance.

He understood that the existence of shot and counter-shot was all in the past. He had dwelt in a land of strange, squalling **upheavals.** Now he had come forth. He had been where there was red of blood and black of passion. Now he was escaped. His first thoughts were given to rejoicings at this fact.

Later he began to study his deeds, his failures, and his achievements. He had come fresh from scenes where many of his usual ways of looking back had been idle. He had proceeded sheeplike from them. He struggled to collect all his acts.

At last they marched before him clearly. From his present viewpoint, he was able to look upon them as a spectator. He could criticize them with some correctness. His new condition had already defeated certain sympathies.

Regarding his procession of memory, he felt gleeful and unregretting. In it, his public deeds were paraded in great and shining **prominence.** Those performances which had been witnessed by his fellows marched now in wide purple and gold.

His deeds took various turns. They went gaily with music. It was a pleasure to watch these things. He spent delightful minutes viewing the gold-coated images of memory. He saw that he was good. He recalled with a thrill of joy the respectful comments of his fellows upon his conduct.

Nevertheless, the ghost of his flight from the first battle appeared to him and danced. There were small shoutings in his brain about these matters. For a moment he blushed. The light of his soul flickered with shame.

A spirit of reproach came to him. There loomed the dogging memory of the tattered soldier. He had been gored by bullets and faint for blood. But he had fretted, concerning an imagined wound in another. He had loaned his last of strength and intellect to the tall soldier. And, blind with weariness and pain, he had been deserted on the field.

For an instant, a miserable chill of sweat was upon the youth. He thought he might be detected in the thing. He stood **persistently** before his vision. And he released a cry of sharp irritation and pain.

His friend turned. "What's the matter, Henry?" he demanded. The youth's reply was an outburst of deep red oaths.

He marched along the little branch-hung roadway among his chattering companions. This vision of cruelty brooded over him. It clung near him always and darkened his view of these deeds in purple and gold. It didn't matter which way his thoughts turned. They were followed by the somber ghost of the desertion in the fields.

He looked secretly at his companions. He felt sure that they must see in his face evidences of this pursuit. But they were plodding in ragged formation. They discussed with quick tongues the accomplishments of the late battle.

"Oh, if a man should come up and ask me, I'd say we got a damn good lickin'."

"Lickin'—in your eye! We ain't licked, sonny. We're goin' down here a ways. Then, we'll swing around and come in behind 'em."

"Oh, hush, with your comin' in behind 'em. I've seen all of that I want to. Don't tell me about comin' in behind—"

"Bill Smithers, he says he'd rather been in ten hundred battles than been in that helluva hospital. He says they got shootin' in the nighttime. Shells are dropped plumb among 'em in the hospital. He says such hollerin' he never see."

"Hasbrouck? He's the best officer in this here regiment. He's a whale."

"Didn't I tell you we'd come around in behind 'em? Didn't I tell you so? We—"

"Oh, shut your mouth!"

For a time, the memory of the tattered man remained. It chased all joy from the youth's veins. He saw his vivid error. He was afraid that it would stand before him all his life.

He took no share in the chatter of his comrades. Nor did he look at them or know them, save when he felt sudden suspicion. He thought they were seeing his thoughts. He thought they were **scrutinizing** each detail of the scene with the tattered soldier.

Yet gradually he mustered force to put the sin at a distance. At last his eyes seemed to open to some new ways. He found that he could look back upon the brass and bombast[1] of his earlier beliefs and see them truly. He was gleeful when he discovered that he now despised them.

With this conviction came a store of assurance. He felt a quiet manhood. It was not aggressive, but of sturdy and strong blood. He knew that he would no more shrink before his guides wherever they should point.

He had been to touch the great death. And he found that, after all, it was but the great death. He was a man.

So it came to pass that he trudged from the place of blood and anger. And his soul changed. Peacefully, he came from hot plowshares[2] to hopes of clover. And it was as if hot plowshares were not. Scars faded as flowers.

It rained. The procession of weary soldiers became a raggedy train. They were depressed and muttering. They marched with **churning** effort in a trough of liquid brown mud under a low, wretched sky.

Yet the youth smiled. He saw that the world was a world for him, though many discovered it to be made of oaths and walking sticks. He had rid himself of the red sickness of battle. The hot nightmare was in the past.

He had been an animal, blistered and sweating, in the heat and pain of war. He turned now with a lover's thirst to images of serene skies, fresh meadows, and cool brooks. He thought of a life of soft and eternal peace.

Over the river, a golden ray of sun came through the masses of heavy rain clouds.

[1]Bombast is pompous or proud speech.
[2]A plowshare is the cutting blade of a plow. This mention of *hot plowshares* refers to the Middle Ages when people often underwent an "ordeal by fire." This was a kind of test which could involve grasping a hot piece of iron. Here, Henry has survived the battle experiences, his "ordeal by fire."

CIVIL WAR ARMY ORGANIZATION

COMPANY — 100 Soldiers

REGIMENT — 1,000 Soldiers (10 Companies)

BRIGADE — 3,000 - 5,000 Soldiers (3 - 5 Regiments)

DIVISION — 10,000+ Soldiers (2 - 5 Brigades)

ARMY CORPS — 20,000+ Soldiers (2 or more Divisions)

FULL ARMY — 40,000+ Soldiers (2 or more Army Corps)

ARMY RANKINGS

Note: Rankings are from highest to lowest.

Commissioned (Officers)

General of the Army
General
Lieutenant General
Major General
Brigadier General
Colonel
Lieutenant Colonel
Major
Captain
First Lieutenant
Second Lieutenant

Noncommissioned (Enlisted Men and Women)

Sergeant Major of the Army
Command Sergeant Major
Sergeant Major
First Sergeant
Master Sergeant
Sergeant First Class
Staff Sergeant
Sergeant
Corporal
Private First Class
Private